All The Lonely Boys in New York

All the Lonely Boys in New York

A Novel By Jeffrey F. Barken

MONOLOGGING.ORG

Monologging Press
New York City
Copyright © 2015
by Jeffrey F. Barken
Monologging.org

This one is for Mom & Dad

PART I

(In Which Nothing Goes As Planned)

5:30 P.M., Wednesday, March 5, 2008.

*"Watch-ing Mydilda, Wash-ing her dildo...
You'll come a watch-ing Mydilda with me?"*

Boy, my mind was busy. That dirty song was stuck in my head and it wasn't even dark yet. Blame the neighbor, our lonely friend, "Mydilda," had left her curtains open again. The girl lay naked on her bed, her blue wand inserted between her legs.

I'd gone out to the fire escape to smoke a cigarette. I could see everything. Mydilda was hardly beautiful, but there was something calming about her lust. *"And she came, and she cried, and she thought about her dildo-long,"* I hummed, reminded of burly Ethan's mad-drunken antics the night he made up all the lyrics. He would love to know that Mydilda was out there on the eve of our attack. Perhaps this was her way of blessing the mission.

I watched the girl caress her breasts and quiver, but I was too nervous to feel aroused. The stub of my cigarette burned my fingertips. I went back inside.

Too bad I couldn't call anyone. Professor Murphy was very clear. Phone calls on the night of the "operation" were forbidden. Murphy was paranoid. He'd confiscated everyone's phones before they left. "We can't make calls or we'll leave a trail for the Feds," he warned. Then he encouraged violence. "Remember Fallujah and Tora Bora? Your countrymen abandoned you. They protested against your brave fight. Time to turn their heads, lads. Show them what this war has done to you and the country. Our success depends on your faith in your comrades. Destroy the recruitment station. Bring chaos to the streets. The 2008 election must be a referendum on the war."

That was the rhetoric the old man was spouting in his Irish brogue, and everybody was committed. Earlier, I'd watched Murphy's crew of veterans and anarchists shake hands one last time. They armed themselves with automatic weapons and explosives, prayed for luck and left their phones on the card table. Ghosts. I could feel them disappearing. They were suicidal terrorists riding downtown to blow up Times Square.

"That's another thing," Murphy said as he supervised their preparations. "You're to open fire, then blend in. The only thing you'll need is a Metro card. Remember, timing is everything."

On their way out, Murphy gave each of them subway fare and a digital watch that had the time synchronized with his own. Then he shook their hands and told them they were heroes.

The pile of phones made me nervous. My job was "secretary." I was supposed to watch over the apartment and record calls. If one of the boys cowered, Professor Murphy threatened to investigate and make retribution. He'd kill anyone who interfered.

What shook me up was the number of people who had already phoned. Everyone was looking for my old friend, Ari. He was supposed to lead one end of the attack. Had he left his post? I didn't know, and I worried about him. After all, he was the only one I really cared about. If it weren't for Ari, I would never have come back to New York. The longer I waited in that stuffy apartment, the more I wanted to flee, seek Ari out and save him from making a mistake. Anxious for news, I glued my eyes to the big screen television that was flickering in the living room.

Madness. There was no way to justify the violence about to erupt. We'd made a pact. "Death to traitors," we agreed, as though we were boys playing pirates. Nobody had taken the blood contract seriously at first, but then the mood changed. Now everyone was behaving unpredictably.

I wasn't sure any of them would go through with the attack, but I was preparing myself for the worst. I flipped through the channels. Channel 8 showed "Friends," Channel 17, "Seinfeld." AMC featured an old Jimmy Stewart movie. Wolf Blitzer squawked on CNN. I clinched the brow of that leather fedora I'd picked up downtown, drummed my fingers on the table, and sang the damn refrain: *"Watch-ing My-dil-da, Wash-ing her dildo...."*

Waiting for Broadway to detonate was a restless trick. All I'd wanted was to apologize to Ari. Maybe I couldn't imagine him forgiving me. Aside from saying "sorry," I knew I'd failed. Everything was wrong.

Listen to my damned apology: "Idle in September," the book I'd been writing since the summer seemed like a lost cause now. I'd started writing because we all felt stuck. I wanted to save Ari's optimism, but I'd been shortsighted and insincere. What I'd written was a waste. Nothing could sway Ari's radical opinions about the wars or the economy. He was utterly devoted to Professor Murphy and fixated on causing chaos in Times Square. I should have walked away when I had the chance.

There'd been signs. How many outrageous conspiracy films had I endured? How many traitorous lectures? Professor Murphy preached that America was in deep decline. He cursed politicians and capitalists, decreeing that our soldiers were sent on a fool's crusade. Now veterans were misunderstood if not shunned for their service. A global catastrophe was imminent. Terror and widespread financial instability loomed. If we could stop the war, Murphy asserted, we could wrest power from the bureaucrats in Washington and save the country.

I clenched my fists, wanting to yell. In light of my comrades' lofty idealism, I wondered if I didn't feel a little left behind on that big night. Everyone I knew was going straight to hell, and I wanted to follow. I thought I at least deserved a better title. Secretary? That pussy-word pissed me off. I was more involved than that. Guilty as charged.

All at once it hit me. None of them might come back. What would happen to this place? I wondered about all the bits and pieces we had collected that year. There was a tall palm tree in the corner, a cactus on a shelf, a garden of herbs and different potted flowers by the window. There was the record player and the vinyl collection that Ari and I had painstakingly gathered, used furniture we had taken off the street, and, of course, the professor's antique player piano, standing prominently in the next room.

"The walls are yours," Murphy promised at one of our first meetings. Nobody understood his invitation until he kicked off the mural project himself. "Do we still believe the Beatles?" he wrote in permanent marker across the white, bathroom door. "Yes or no?" Murphy demanded. "Leave your mark."

Nine lost and lonely boys hiding in apartment 2W, 517 East 75th Street. Three rooms aligned like railroad cars, the walls cluttered with graffiti and toxic slogans. These rooms were witness to our plans. I don't know when the turning point came, but as we "organized," we ventured down a strange and irreversible path. Everyone relied on the initial camaraderie of the group for a sense that nights of desperate drinking could help us escape the reality of a bad economy. Nobody realized how we were all the time digesting virulent rhetoric, coalescing around points of anger and committing to a terrorist plot. On the contrary, Professor Murphy empowered us to rise above the challenges we faced. He'd opened the mouths of shocked, muted veterans and we believed the meetings were therapeutic.

The pastel mural celebrated free speech. Everyone had contributed to the project. We'd drawn a city scene. Taxis, skyscrapers, green Central Park, bright lights and shadowy alleys. The project pulsed distraction. Countless nights we'd reveled in creative pleasure. We smeared our wasting energy across the central wall in color, forgot our oldest ambitions, blamed our parents for our hardship, and surrendered to Murphy's rage.

I sat on the couch and changed channels: Back to that Jimmy Stewart movie, "Vertigo," in time for the scene where Stewart follows the blonde, bewitched girl to the museum.

Someone knocked.

I turned off the television.

Silence. I fumbled for the German Luger my grandfather left me, crept toward the door and looked through the peephole. In the hallway, a man stood wrapped in a heavy wool coat. He coughed twice and came closer, covering my view.

"Myles, open up. It's me," my visitor whispered.

Jesus, it was Lee Callick. I unlocked the door. Lee stumbled in, shivering.

"Are you hurt? What's happened? You're early. Nothing should have happened yet."

Lee's broad posture was caving. His straight, buzzed hair was matted down with sweat.

"What are you doing here? You have to get back to your post. We signed the pact. Remember?" I blabbered.

"I can't do it, Myles," he said, fighting tears. He would have stood there crying if I didn't tell him to sit down and offer to brew some sobering tea.

While I was in the kitchen, Lee turned on the TV.

"Don't watch the news," I said, handing him his steaming mug and changing the channel back to my movie. "Wait till later."

Lee rubbed his bloodshot eyes. "Do you think Murphy will kill me?" he asked.

"Drink," I said. He hadn't touched his tea.

Lee sipped. "Will he?" he asked again.

"Of course not," I said, lying. I was all too familiar with Murphy's violent streak.

Lee told me what twists and turns his mind had taken as he rode his bicycle downtown. At the corner of 56th Street and 7th Avenue, he'd gotten off his bike and walked the rest of the way. Suddenly, he was shocked by how many people were on the streets. "I couldn't do it," he cried. "I couldn't shoot them."

He owed the rest of his complex to his mother. He had been thinking about her all day. What would she say when she learned her two sons were terrorists? Lee couldn't handle the question. He simply wasn't up to murder. At the Starbucks across from his post in Times Square, he broke down. Then he took the subway back uptown. His bike was still chained to a signpost on Broadway.

"I'm sorry Myles," Lee said. "I don't want to put you in danger, but I didn't know where else to go."

"That's alright, Lee," I said, patting his back. "We're in this together. Tell me, did you see anyone else as you were leaving? What about your brother, Dylan? Did you see Ari anywhere? Does anybody know you've quit your post?"

He didn't know.

"Why don't you take a shower? I suggested. "You'll feel better once you've cleaned up."

After some coaxing, Lee followed my advice. I went to the closet in the far room to fetch a towel. That was Professor Murphy's office. Usually he'd lock the door if he was out, but tonight he'd given me the key. I let myself inside.

Another shock. Murphy's heavy oak desk was missing from its place by the window. The couch and leather chairs were gone, and all the bookshelves were empty. Despite the lacking furnishings, Murphy evidently expected the boys would want to shower when they returned. He'd left a stack of clean towels on a small wicker chair in the corner.

I had to think the puzzle through. The last few days were so busy, when did the old man find time to move his things out? Never mind. Lee was searching for his cell phone in the pile on the living room table.

"Lee, don't!" I yelled, running to grab the phone from him. "You can't."

"Let me call my mom," he begged. "She's worried. Can't I call her?"

What difference did it make? The operation was fucked now anyway. The poor kid only wanted to call his mom.

"Fine," I said. "But pull yourself together and make it quick. No big confessions."

Lee thanked me, wiped his sweaty face with the cloth and limped into the other room.

The cold night swept in through the open window on the fire escape. I didn't want to eavesdrop, but it was hard not to overhear. Lee's whining was unbearable. He was a big, strong kid. He worked construction down at Ground Zero, and he worshiped the cult of honorable manhood. How many times had I heard him pledge his life to Murphy's cause? He was supposed to be willing, "perfectly willing." Now, here he was, breaking the pact and crying to mom? I wondered who'd show up next and what shape they'd be in. The night was all too young.

The Failed Apology
(May 2007)

Sirens! I still couldn't believe my ears. Everyone in the city was screaming English. Only two months had passed since I'd returned to the States. The sight of English billboards and the conversations I overheard in the street were overwhelming. Swarms of gossiping, galloping strangers made my head spin, disrupting all the peace I'd gained abroad.

It was Joel's fault I'd ended up in Brooklyn again. We'd formed a habit of hanging out. Aside from Ari, he was the only person from home I still knew in the city. The pointy-nosed kid had put me up for a week when I first got back from Israel. Often drugged, he'd been a decent friend. Joel liked to play music, and he always smoked me up for free. Usually I was happy for his company, but lately our binges had been excessive. Especially when we celebrated the publication of my story, *Around the Mountain*, in the New Yorker. The piece was about Ari and my trip out west in 2003, on the eve of the Iraq war. A lot had happened to us on the road. When we got home our lives felt out of our control. I'd written everything down and submitted the memoir, never expecting success.

"Why do you want to find Ari anyway? Can't you look him up on the Internet?" Joel would ask, baffled that I'd come all the way back to New York to reconnect with an old friend.

Luckily, I could always blow Joel off easy. "I owe the guy an apology," I'd tell him between joints or lines. "That's all. I want a fresh start."

The way I saw it, there was no need to tell Joel the whole story; how I'd broken up Ari and his fiancée when I slept with Melissa, then skipped town. Not that Joel would think any less of me for having betrayed a friend. On the contrary, he enjoyed cheering for scoundrels. But I didn't want his apathy to compromise my determination. I'd come back to do one thing: set the record straight and apologize to my friend. Ari was the only one who needed to know.

Famous last words. The morning I finally found Ari, I woke up on Joel's couch with one, big, New York headache. I stumbled out of his apartment and wandered around until I came to the promenade overlooking the East River. There, I slept an hour on a bench. When I woke, the headache was worse. The city across the river gleamed in the sun. Off to my right, the Brooklyn Bridge stretched like a triumphal arch above the water.

I gave the day up for lost and walked aimlessly down Pierrepont, past the children's playground and an ice cream truck. I stared deep into the tall windows on the brownstones, admiring the chandeliers, the portraits on the walls, and the elaborate wooden staircases. I thought I could hear the saxophone from the *Cosby Show* intro ringing in my ears. Then I turned the corner and saw him.

Ari was in a hurry. He waited to enter a tall apartment building at the corner. I watched him check his watch and wipe his brow with his sleeve. Maybe he'd gained weight? His face was rounder than before, his ears stuck out under his glasses, and his sideburns were long and frizzy. I thought he looked good. Ari rang the bell again and searched his phone for a number.

"There's a stranger," I said, coming up behind him.

Startled, Ari turned around. "I was wondering when you'd turn up," he said. "I heard you were in the city."

"I heard the same," I mumbled back.

Ari was breathing hard. He scratched under his glasses and took two puffs from an inhaler he kept in his pocket.

"I read your story," he said.

"Don't worry. It's not *all* about us," I replied. "I didn't think I'd ever see you again."

I was relieved when Ari's sister, Zoey, appeared at the door, interrupting us. She, too, looked more or less the same. She was short and had a round face. Her dark, wet, hair hung over her shoulder in a thick braid.

"Myles!" she said, flashing that incredible smile that she and all her siblings shared. "Are you here to help? I haven't seen you in years." She threw her arms around me. Then she turned toward her brother. "I was *so* mad at you this morning," she scolded. "But you found Myles?"

Zoey was moving to a new apartment and Ari's friends had bailed on helping with the U-Haul.

"Actually, Myles found me," Ari said, looking back and forth at Zoey and me. "He's *not* helping."

"No, that's fine," I said. "I'll help. I don't have any plans."

"Great! *Thank you.* So good to see you," Zoey said, hugging me again.

"Seriously, Myles. You don't have to help," Ari insisted.

"Please?" Zoey begged. "I'm mostly packed. We'll get the truck at one and I'll buy you guys pizza and beer afterward. If Myles helps, the move will go so much faster. ”

"I'm sold." I said.

Ari didn't refuse her offer.

Now I was optimistic that I'd have a chance to talk honestly with Ari. When Zoey led us inside, however, I began to feel like an intruder. After what I'd done to my friend, I had no right to expect such a warm reception from anyone in his family. I'd anticipated Zoey's scorn, but she was as friendly as ever. Could Ari not have told her how I betrayed him?

"Where have you been all this time? It's been ages. *Seriously,* ages," Zoey talked the entire elevator ride up to her apartment. "Ari told me you were in Israel?"

Her apartment was small and square with two bedrooms on opposite ends of a narrow hallway. Other than the couch, a dresser and her industrial-sized laser printer, everything was packed in duffel bags or boxed up. Zoey led us to the kitchen where she made coffee. Discovering a pack of meatballs his sister was leaving behind in the freezer, Ari insisted on microwaving the snack.

The next four hours were an intense scramble but also some of the best fun we'd had together in years. We were racing against time. Picking up the U-Haul was hell. The office was closing early. We had a five o'clock curfew by which to complete the move and return the rental. Otherwise, we had to drive the truck out of the city because it was illegal to park something so large overnight in Brooklyn. Our mission seemed impossible, but we were determined to get the job done.

Back at Zoey's place, Ari and I were soaked in sweat. We took turns charging up and down the stairs. We packed the elevator full of furniture and boxes and sent the cargo down the shaft to the lobby where we loaded the truck. Zoey, meanwhile, kept an eye on the clock, made sure we had water and held doors open for us. We all agreed that we were living out a *Seinfeld* episode.

By the time we got to Zoey's new address, it was already four o'clock. Ari and I swung into action. Our plan was to get everything inside the building, return the truck and then cart Zoey's belongings upstairs. In our haste, there *were* casualties. Several plates and glasses broke and some drawers from Zoey's dresser fell into the street before oncoming traffic. There was a lot of yelling and sweating—the stinky, salty sweat of movers—until we finally finished and Ari raced back to the U-Haul depot to return the truck. I don't want to know how many red lights he ran. Somehow he arrived before the deadline.

Zoey's new apartment was smaller than her last one, but her new roommate—away at work—had already made it cozy. A TV waited in the square living room for Zoey's couch, the pantry was stocked with snacks, and Zoey's bedroom looked out over Jeralman Street. She seemed depressed when we heard the subway rumble underneath us.

As soon as Zoey left to pick up our pizza, I realized this was the first time in two years Ari and I had been alone together. For a while, we were both tense and hardly able to say anything. We took turns going downstairs to bring up the remaining boxes and avoided being in the same room for very long. Then Ari surprised me, grabbing my arm on the stairs.

"Let's check out the roof later," he suggested. "I bet it's one hell of a view."

We bought beer across the street and shared the pizza with Zoey. Afterward, she wanted to start unpacking and said we were free to leave. We quickly said goodbye, darted upstairs, opened the heavy door and walked out into an incredible panorama of New York. On the edge of the rooftop, we sat for hours, downing Brooklyn beer, remembering growing up together in Ithaca, stories from college, and admiring the skyscrapers that glowed across the humid, hazy night.

"Sounds as though you had a great trip," Ari said about my time abroad. "To tell you the truth, I'm jealous." When Ari went to the other side of the air duct to take a piss, I rested my head against the brick wall and asked him about his latest trek out west.

"The drive was very different traveling alone" he said. "Nothing like your story."

Occasionally he'd been bored and lonely on the road, but he said he hadn't had a bad time. He'd seen a lot—the Badlands, Bryce and Zion, then Yosemite. I cringed when Ari admitted that the trip was therapeutic. Initially he had required some convincing, just to move his ass and get the car serviced. Now he credited his younger brother, Jeremy, for encouraging him to make the journey. He said driving west was exactly the escape he needed after things fell through with his fiancée.

"How's Jeremy?" I asked, remembering a smart kid and a good musician.

"He took *your* advice," Ari said, a harsh note in his voice. "Jeremy flew abroad to Ireland about a year ago."

"You keep in touch?"

"Pretty well. We got close after you left."

Our talk droned on into the night.

"Do you remember Professor Murphy?" Ari asked. He was referring to the hideous Irishman whose fiery lectures he'd often drag me to when we were at Cornell. Ari had reconnected with his former advisor. Now, the two of them had organized a counseling group that helped Iraq and Afghanistan war veterans re-adapt to civilian life. Ari said the work was important, and he invited me to attend one of their weekly meetings.

I said I'd try. Ari was skeptical that I'd commit, but he grew optimistic when I told him how close the Upper East Side restaurant I worked at was to the apartment where his group met.

"*Toto's?* Isn't that the Wizard of Oz diner where you can bring your dog?"

I nodded. Ari grinned. At times, the two of us were jovial. I made a lot of toasts, and Ari loosened up as soon as he was drunk. At the base of things, however, it was hard to know where I stood. Ari seemed to enjoy my company, and he was eager to talk. He laughed off my sentimental nostalgia, repeating our old motto from college, "Life moves faster than reason." But he also held back, dropping a dozen hints—fade away smiles and sarcasm—that showed his discomfort with us being friends again.

Maybe I didn't need to say sorry. Perhaps that was Ari's point inviting me up to the roof and choosing to extend the night. He wanted me to know that he was over his ex. He said there was a new girl in his life whom he was crazy about. His brother had become a true and unexpected friend after I left New York. His work with professor Murphy was fulfilling.

Finally, when it was very late, I tried to reason with him. I wanted to catch a subway and save my money, but Ari insisted I take a cab. He put a twenty in my hand and walked me outside. At the corner, where we said goodbye, a mumbled "sorry" escaped my lips. Ari's reaction was so minimal I wondered if he even heard me.

"Home," I told the driver, as I watched Ari stumble into the shadows. "106 and Columbus."

We sped off. The cabby was chatty, but I couldn't concentrate or make conversation. Instead, I kept contemplating my pathetic phrase. Under my breath, "I'm sorry—what I put you through," I repeated the sentence I'd told Ari a dozen times. Nothing had ever felt so incomplete.

8:00 P.M., Wednesday, March 5, 2008.

Lee was still in the other room. He was fidgeting and pacing. I heard him play a little ditty on that old tinny piano—one of the old-time rags Professor Murphy taught him. He played fast, tapping ringing notes high and low along the scale. Then the music stopped. The latch on the piano bench creaked open and slammed shut. The trundle underneath the cot scratched across the floor. Before I could stand up to see what Lee was looking for, he barged back into the room where I was watching TV.

"We've been robbed!" Lee announced. The big kid took up the whole doorway. "The scrolls are gone. I wanted to play one, but all the music is missing."

Lee ran through the rooms collecting evidence. Furniture had been moved, objects were missing, and appliances were plugged into different outlets. He was in shock.

"Lee!" I yelled, chasing after him and finally cornering him in the kitchen.

"Calm down," I said, shaking him. "We weren't robbed. Professor Murphy moved a few things out. That's all."

Lee turned pale. "Moved out? Why would he do that?"

The only thing I could think of was that the lease for the apartment ran out at the end of the month. "Maybe he wanted to get an early start?" I suggested. I tossed Lee the key to Professor Murphy's empty room so that he could see the missing furniture. When the kid returned, he was clutching something in his hand.

"What did you find?" I asked.

Lee opened his fist, revealing a crumpled two-dollar bill. I examined the side showing the signing of the Declaration of Independence, then the other side's portrait of Jefferson.

"So?" I asked, flipping the bill over twice more. There was nothing remarkable about the money, nothing written or stamped on either side. But Lee was superstitious.

"I found it lying on the floor. You didn't notice? It's for good luck," he said. "Isn't it?"

I put the bill in my pocket and out of Lee's sight. I had no idea what to make of the find.

Trembling, Lee began to mumble. "You're supposed to be here. Not me," he said. "We never made plans for after the attack. We should have, but we didn't. Jesus, Myles, we're a bunch of fools. We're not prepared! But Murphy is. He's got a plan to kill us all."

Independence Day
(July 4, 2007)

I hadn't seen Ari in over a month.

"Toto's, And Your Little Dog Too!" For the sixth time in an endless minute, I caught myself staring at that restaurant sign. When Ari popped his head inside, the obnoxious canine clock was still barking the hour from behind the cashier's counter.

"I like the witch and the cauldron," Ari said, pointing to the far end of the petite East Side diner where all sorts of *Wizard of Oz* collector's memorabilia hung above the bar. Then he asked me if we gave customers green-tinted glasses to achieve the full "Emerald City effect."

I rolled my eyes and shoved a menu in his hands.

There had been a small rush during lunch hour. Afterward, things settled down. I was nervous talking to Ari. I knew my boss was on the prowl for slackers. He'd already yelled at me once for speaking Spanish to the kitchen staff.

"Will you get off in time for the fireworks?" Ari asked.

"Doubtful. I have the long shift. I need the money."

Ari took a step back. "Come to the party at CitiBar tonight," he suggested. "We're all meeting there after the fireworks."

"We?" I inquired.

"Old friends. I think you'll remember some people."

"Can I invite Joel? We were going to meet up."

"Joel from home?"

I nodded.

"I doubt he'll come, but sure. Why not? He will remember some of the guys too. The bar is only a few blocks from here. Drop by. We'll celebrate."

"Sounds good. I'll eat after my shift. Then I'll come."

Satisfied, Ari shook my hand again and strolled off. Before the door closed, I could feel my boss, Carlo, breathing down my neck.

"Wha'd he want?" Carlo demanded, slicking his straight black hair.

"Nothing," I answered. "He wasn't hungry."

Carlo pointed toward the stack of folded yellow menus.

"You give'm one?" he asked. He spoke more like a New Yorker and less like an Italian whenever he was worried about money. "Make sure y'give-out my menus. Give'em'out and let people know we deliver. You got that? Good."

The little guy went outside to smoke a cigarette. He was on edge. He'd hired too many waiters, expecting the place to be packed on the holiday. I watched Carlo smoke and pace about out front, his hands buried in his tight jean pockets. Carlo could be moody as hell, but I liked him and I liked the job. I was the host, and except for when Carlo thought he was losing money, he'd treat me like a manager. On top of my pay, I got two free meals out of every shift.

Still, it had been an odd stretch. I knew there was tension brewing among the waiters and kitchen staff. First of all, it was like Babel back there. Everyone spoke more Spanish than English, and Carlo hated it when his orders got lost. Second, business had slowed since the spring. Already we could feel the coming recession. The Wall Street hotshots who used to sit at the bar, order steak and eggs and bitch about the skeptics who were bearing the market, had disappeared. Fewer families were coming in for Sunday brunch. If the slump continued, somebody would get sacked. That was obvious.

In the meantime, I didn't mind when my shift was slow. That afternoon, there was never a line, only the steady stream of couples looking for a booth where they could share omelets and play Footsie under the table. Hung-over college girls came too. They picked away at greasy food, stressed and gossiped about men. Most of the chatter came from the two families having brunch together in the back. Parents tried to speak above their screaming babies while servers tripped over the Hummer-sized double baby carriages they'd parked next to their table.

When Carlo's wife, Sienna, came by to pick him up later that afternoon, she saw how barren the place was. Concerned, she ran her bejeweled fingers through her long black hair and waved to her husband. Next, she took two packets of sugar and spread them along the sidewalk outside, making a trail leading to the restaurant.

"Is dolce. When customer smells sugar, he gets hungry," she said, explaining the old, Italian wives' tale trick to me.

I smiled, watching Carlo and Sienna argue in Italian. Their love made me jealous. They never passed each other without either bickering hopelessly or exchanging a squeeze or a pinch or some starry-eyed look.

On his way out, Carlo slipped me an extra twenty.

"Keep an eye on everybody," he said. "I'm trusting you."

The sun went down around nine that night. I guess there were fireworks across the Hudson, but I couldn't hear or see them. On my break, I called Joel. He was at some rooftop party in Hell's Kitchen, and he was stoned.

"Will you come to that bar with me?" I asked. "I'm off in an hour."

"You're meeting Ari?" he burped, "Ari from high school? No. I don't want to see *him.*"

Joel sounded a mess, but I couldn't tell why he was reluctant to meet Ari. "Call me if you change your mind," I said, blowing him off.

An hour later my shift ended. Starved, I asked the salad guy to whip me up a chicken wrap with fries while I counted out the cash register. I didn't remember that twenty-dollar bill my boss gave me until I was outside, fishing through my pockets on the way to CitiBar. Thinking of the money I owed in rent, I tried to convince myself I shouldn't spend anything, but then again, I was seeing Ari. I owed him a round. No matter what, I always owed him.

My throat stopped burning from the first shot of whiskey barely in time to take another. Boy, Ari had changed. I'd never seen him drink so hard. In college, I used to have to talk him into things. Now he was leading the charge, and I couldn't keep up.

When I finally got Ari's attention, I had nothing worthwhile to say.

"Where's your girl?" I yelled over the bar chatter and rock music. "You never told me her name."

"Hailey," Ari answered.

"I want to meet her."

"She isn't here."

Ari shook his head to the music. I realized he probably didn't want to talk about his girlfriend. Not with me anyway. But he didn't take it badly that I had asked. He was busy ordering a drink for a tall guy with a newsy cap and black spider web tattoo spun around his elbow. The guy had bleached blonde hair and arms like Popeye.

When he turned toward me, I was stunned. "Mav, is that you?" I asked.

"Myles?" Ethan Mav said, grinning. "What's happening?"

"I'm trying to remember the last time I saw you. Was it New Years Eve, 2004?"

Slowly the facts came back to me. Ethan dropped out of college and joined the army when the war started. He'd been to Iraq twice in four years. The last time I'd seen him he'd spilled beer everywhere and bragged to everyone that he would kill a few Iraqis.

Ethan obviously remembered his delusional agenda before he joined the army and the scene he'd made at the party. "I was an ass then. Forget about that, will you?" he asked. "The damn war will be over soon enough. Once we get somebody competent in the White House, anyway."

Ethan was interrupted when Alan, Ari's freshman year college roommate, appeared behind me. He hadn't changed a bit. Clean-shaven, big nose, dark parted hair, and dark eyes. We shook hands and ordered shots. That seemed to be the only way to handle a reunion.

"I'm right on track," Alan boasted about his career. After finishing his degree, he'd gone into politics. Now he was working for AIPAC as a lobbyist while he finished paying off his enormous college loans.

Alan's girlfriend, Rachel, was fantastic. A brunette and a good flirt, she put her hand on my shoulder when she wanted to try my drink and blushed whenever Alan squeezed her waist or said something dirty. Rachel asked me if I had any blow. "I don't usually go in for the hard stuff," she said, a bit embarrassed. "But it's the Fourth. I thought I'd be crazy."

"And patriotic," Alan joked.

I offered to get them in touch with Joel. He always had something lying around. But they didn't want to leave the bar to meet him.

Next, Ari and Alan introduced me to two of their other friends—a lawyer and an investment banker.

"Partners in crime?" I asked. They laughed together.

"We do our part to keep life interesting," Sam, the lawyer said. They were the only two guys in suits at the bar, and they had that square, 1980's, Risky Business look. Jim, the banker, was almost bald. Sam was younger. Dark hair, fat cheeks, he thought everything was too funny.

A frown passed over Jim's face. He didn't find Sam's joke amusing. "Business is bad," he admitted. "There's a lot of inflation and debt. The situation could easily get worse."

Never mind. The two of them put together their glasses to toast turning the slump around, ending the wars and the coming election. Taking me aside, Sam told me about his wife and kid.

"She doesn't know about these parties," he said, grinning. "You'd keep secrets from your wife too, wouldn't you? I'm supposed to be in Philly for a meeting with a client tonight."
Then he asked me if I wanted to babysit his kid. He said he paid twenty an hour and that he'd take good care of me.

I said I'd consider the offer. I didn't know if I'd be any good with kids. After that, Sam lost interest. I started to wander away. Back at the bar, I met another veteran named Chris. He wore a green Army shirt, and he kept rearranging a series of war scene sketches he'd drawn on paper napkins.

"They're no good," he complained about the noisy band. "Everybody is still playing Vietnam music. Our war is different and needs its own sound. Something new. This music doesn't come close to capturing what we experienced over there."

He told me about the desert they rode tanks across to capture Baghdad. He talked endlessly about the "Surge" and all the generals he'd never trusted. When he complained redundantly about the music, I started looking around for a means of escaping the conversation.

Thank God for Dylan. He showed up with his kid brother Lee and interrupted. I hadn't seen Dylan since Ari and I drove west together. We'd met him out in Yellowstone and given him a ride back East. Lee told me briefly about his construction job down at Ground Zero.

Dylan ordered us all a round. Shots, shots, shots. They kept on coming and I was plastered. Too many people were mixing up with too many memories. When Ari led me through the bar and set me loose on the dance floor, I fell into the arms of a girl I'd flirted with earlier. We started dancing. The girl's blonde hair was tied up in dreadlocks. She was calling everyone out for their faults.

"There goes Ethan, always acting the big war hero," she said, holding a hand over my ear to cover the secrets she yelled above the music. "Watch out if he tells you about his injury. He lies. Ethan's unit wasn't ambushed. He slit his wrist to get out of the army."

Next she pointed across the room to where Ethan was making out with a plain-faced girl I vaguely remembered from high school. "Good thing he still has Josie to cheat on. That girl is about the only thing holding that maniac together."

Her name was Margot. She was an NYU student and she wouldn't stop begging me to join in an upcoming war protest that she and her friends were organizing.

"Please come," she said, drawing a flyer out of her outrageously pink backpack. We made out in the back of the bar for a bit. She didn't shave, and her armpit hair escaped her checkered dress. That was unusual. I kissed her hard and passionate, sucking on her lower lip and rolling my tongue against hers. I pressed myself close to her and made sure she could feel my erection through my shorts, but I went numb when we bumped up against the scuzzy black wall. I knew I was too drunk to go much further and, besides, I felt guilty hooking up around Ari. It made a bad new impression.

Another sloppy kiss and a squeeze, then I let go of the girl. Dizzy, I stumbled toward the back table and sat down. Ari spotted me sitting by myself. I was falling asleep. He brought me a glass of water. Then he pointed out Professor Murphy. The short, balding, big-nosed man, with bushy eyebrows was sitting in the center of a group on the other side of the bar. Ari explained that Murphy had personally opened up a tab for the night and that we were all invited to drink at his expense.

"This is the group I've been telling you about. You see? We have fun," Ari said, patting me on the back. "Professor Murphy takes good care of his boys. We always come here after meetings."

When I put my head down on the table and closed my eyes, Ari helped me up and walked me outside.

"You haven't changed a bit, Myles," he said, smiling as he stood on the curb to hail a cab. "You're still a cheap drunk."

This time I didn't take his money. I had Carlo's twenty crumpled in my pocket.

"I'll come to your next meeting," I promised, before shutting the car door.

"Good."

"And, Ari, will I ever meet her?"

"You mean Hailey?"

Ari smiled and backed away. "We'll see," he said. "Happy Fourth of July, Myles. Get some rest."

Ashamed I'd had the nerve to meddle in his personal life, I watched Ari disappear into the bar and gave the cabby my address. The meter was already running.

We'd hardly driven two blocks before I was nauseous. I begged to get out, angering the cabby.

"You say you want West Side, then you switch. Ten dollars!" The Chinese driver demanded. "You waste my time."

I threw my twenty at him and asked for ten back. No sooner had my feet hit the curb then the cab sped away. I was a block from the Metropolitan Museum. When I got there, I sat for a while on the marble steps, waiting for my stomach to stop churning and my vision to steady. Then I wandered into Central Park.

Beautiful summer. I could smell the warm pollen and the fresh mulch piled around bushes and blooming trees. Here and there, I spied secret gardens and that Egyptian obelisk rising above the shrubs. I walked towards the softball fields on a path I knew was well lit. In the middle, there was an open view of midtown. Despite the peace and quiet, I was restless.

Poetry is dead! I drew bitter conclusions as I contemplated the difficulty of writing a book about Ari. The trouble was I couldn't connect one thought to the next. I needed a first line, something describing Ari and me when we were at our best. Something clever.

There was a rustling in the trashcan behind me. A raccoon climbed out of his lunch bin and scattered for the woods. Nearby, a wire fence ran around the softball fields. I scraped my leg when I clumsily hopped the barrier, limped to second base and sat cross-legged in front of the glowing city. There was a little blood on my leg. I dabbed it with my shirt. At least I didn't feel like retching anymore. Closing my eyes, I began to relax.

Few parks are perfect, but I'd always felt I could find the whole world inside Central Park. Suddenly, I could hear my breathing, and I felt the humidity. There I was, alone at night in New York's fantasy land, ready to depart into my fiction. As eager as I was to begin writing, I knew I was hardly in the mood for dreaming up plots. Before I put pen to paper, I needed to discover the theme at the heart of the book, the pulse of energy and imagery that would reveal and revive my friendship with Ari. Above all, I needed to understand why it was so important to me that he'd accept my apology.

I kept thinking about Ari's friends. I knew almost all of them. A few had been to the wars. The banker and the lawyer played a strange role. The girls I'd met seemed jealous or superficial. That old professor looked angry. Everyone taken together made Ari such a new mystery and New York a confounding swarm of moods and energy.

Who was I to tell a story? Where was Dickens when we needed him? Who else could have judged the times with better balance? I figured it wasn't possible. Poetry *was* dead. I thought poets were all obscure, and that satire was man's cruelest invention. The more I convinced myself of this convenient literary theory, the more I began to doubt myself. What was worse, I hated that my instinct was to write my feelings away instead of explaining them to Ari in person.

After all, how could I write about my affair with his fiancée without hurting him again? I remembered Melissa. *Sweet Melissa*, we called her. I could replay the scene exactly. Summer of 2004: The three of us went up to Montreal for a long weekend. Melissa was dancing at the Jazz festival.

The girl was crazy-wild, but Ari loved her. She had him wrapped around her finger the way he'd feel the need to buy her presents on all occasions. Flowers, chocolates, spontaneous weekend trips, hotels and concert tickets. He wanted her to "feel like a star." That was how he explained the extravagance to me, and he refused to be talked out of spoiling her. I knew the only reason he ever wanted me to tag along to her performances was so that I'd keep him company when she was on stage dancing. Otherwise, he'd be absolutely lonely in his theatre seat, wondering if Melissa really needed him for anything.

Still, we had fun so long as the excitement lasted. That summer in Montreal, the drunken French were singing and dancing in the streets. Melissa looked stunning. Her short black hair curled up—feisty. She wore a black skirt and leotard, her hard nipples showing through the thin, stretchy fabric. Before she went on stage, Ari and I stole away to smoke a joint in an alley. We could hear the crowd cheering. Melissa was all we could talk about.

"She looks good, doesn't she?" Ari asked. "Look at that body. I don't deserve a girl like that..."

He was always a little insecure about Melissa's figure, but I would encourage him. At night, we indulged our every whim. When Melissa brought us to a strip club, we didn't protest. She said she wanted to see how we'd react. First she bought me a lap dance from one of the dancers. Then she gave Ari one herself.

Pin her up, she was a fantasy. After that we both spoiled Melissa. We blew money all over town, at bars and restaurants. We took turns picking up the tab, pretending we were Butch and Sundance, flush after hitting a bank. Then we went shopping. Big bags of clothes and souvenirs piled up. The once-in-a-lifetime binge had to run its course.

On the third day of the festival, things took a turn. We'd made the mistake of sharing a hotel suite. From my bed on the couch I'd wake up to a hangover and the sound of Ari and Melissa either fucking or fighting. The mood grew heavier as tempers flared. When Ari stormed off at lunch, leaving me alone with Melissa, that's when she started testing me. How sneaky. Her foot covered mine. Her voice teased. Everything had changed.

If I could remember Montreal, then I could remember the rest. As soon as we were back in New York that summer, I knew things would never be the same. Ari was involved with Kerry's campaign for President, a losing idealistic battle that was pushing him to the limit. He worked eighty-hour weeks, and all he could talk about was politics. That drove Melissa crazy. He hardly had any time to see her or help plan their wedding, and she couldn't stand hearing about the corrupt Bush administration and 9/11. She started playing games to make him jealous.

Their ups and downs were ceaseless and they'd both call me to vent frustrations. Somehow, I only grew closer to Melissa. She asked me to edit the resumes and cover letters she was sending to dance troupes. Once, when Ari was busy, I helped her move to a new sublet. Afterward, we grabbed a drink. She was livid, not that Ari had neglected to help, but because he didn't want her to move in with him until after the election and the wedding. Soon I became her confidant. She'd ask me to critique her dancing and insisted I discredit anything Ari said about her style. She didn't even want him at her performances anymore. She wanted me.

I didn't make love to her the first time I spent the night at her apartment. Not the second time either. The first few times I slept in her bed we only cuddled and talked, but it felt good and I couldn't stop. I craved her body incessantly, and I fell into her trap. Then I had to face Ari.

I felt like screaming. The grass was dewy, and I was cold and wet. I leapt to my feet. I wanted to be out of the park, home and safe in a bed. I knew my midnight reverie was a waste of time. I'd gone full circle recounting all that Melissa torture, and I hadn't evolved my idea for my book about Ari one bit. All I had discovered was that I wanted my friend back. The story was hiding in my memories.

Then I reconsidered. My writing, after all, had always been about friendship. Ever try to explain a man's loyalties? The strangest elements in our behavior all stem from our desire to make friends. Friends for no reason. Friends by chance. Friends out of boredom. Friends on purpose. Once a connection is made, the tests of time ensue. The process reveals our hope that wherever we are, whatever we are doing, we'll make friends, and this time it will be forever.

I wasn't prepared to believe that the pinnacle moment for Ari and me—the true test of our friendship—had occurred on that trip to Montreal three years ago. We'd grown up together, and it seemed unfair that all our childhood optimism was spoiled. If I could write the book, then perhaps I could forget how I'd wronged Ari and so could he. All I needed to do was spend a little time like money and prove to him that my apology was sincere.

Finally, I'd found the phrase I'd been searching for all night. "It doesn't matter what you spend it on," Ari once said, after fighting with Melissa. "Sometimes the best way to start feeling better is to spend a little money."

That sounded like the first line of a novel.

8:33 P.M., Wednesday, March 5, 2008

BZZZT! BZZZT! BZZZT! BZZZT!

Who was ringing the bell? I was in the bathroom, writing a dirty text to my roommate, Nathalie.

"Lee, don't touch the buzzer," I yelled into the other room.

The bell rang relentlessly, but I had to finish typing my message. Nathalie had written to me about new lingerie and a "little scene" she wanted to practice.

I was aroused. "Sorry doll, tied up at work," I frantically spelled out my reply. "Are you touching yourself? What's my line before I kiss you?"

God, I loved Nat's acting games. We shared a fantasy and were always pretending.

There, I sent the message and hid my phone in my pocket. The doorbell rang again. I opened the bathroom door. Lee was pacing back and forth in the hallway, biting his nails.

"Make yourself useful," I said. "Check the camera." I didn't mean to snap at Lee, but I was sick of coaching him through traumas. Lee followed me down the hall. In the middle room, we turned on the monitor for the security camera. There was no one there. Whoever rang the bell was already inside.

"Do you think it's the cops?"

"Shut up," I said. Next thing I knew we were hiding behind the curtains in Professor Murphy's empty room, searching the street below for NYPD. All we could see were the yellow lights from the Con Ed plant and a few parked cars.

We scrambled for our guns and crept back down the hall.

"I'll check the peephole," I whispered to Lee. "Cover me."

"Ari? Myles? Please!" Our visitor banged on the door.

I stalled, recognizing Hailey's voice. I couldn't decide if I should say anything. I had no idea what she knew about Ari's work with Professor Murphy. One look inside the apartment would wise her up to our conspiracy. I didn't need her getting emotional or calling the cops. At least not until I was sure Ari was safe and innocent.

Hailey wouldn't stop pounding her fist against the wood. She freaked when my phone beeped with another message from Nathalie.

"Myles, what the hell is going on? Where's Ari? Come on! I heard your phone. I know you're there!" Her voice wasn't steady. She'd been crying.

"I hate you, Myles. I fucking hate you. Let me in. Please, I'm scared!" Hailey yelled until she became hoarse. Then she stopped knocking. There was a thud as Hailey sat down on the floor, resting her back against the door.

I squinted through the peephole. I could see the top of Hailey's head and her tangled blonde hair. She was searching in her bag for her phone and cigarettes. I motioned to Lee, mouthing: "Find Ari's cell. On the card table."

Lee made so much noise, I wanted to hit him. Luckily, he managed to turn off the phone before it rang.

Outside, Hailey left a message full of sobs.

"Damn it, love," she cried. "Where are you?"

Hailey
(Late July 2007)

I met Hailey on a muggy Sunday, not long after Ari's Fourth of July party. Joel had come over to my place to play music. He sat in my room, tuning up the instruments. Meanwhile, fine smells wafted inside from the trendy little Italian place downstairs, making us hungry.

My apartment was actually quite spacious. There was a large common area with big windows overlooking the street and two smaller bedrooms. Since Nathalie only came home when she wanted something from me, I took many liberties and often borrowed her things. The only comforts we lacked were decent furniture and air conditioning. For seating in the common room, there was the half-broken rocking chair I'd found on the street, a few stools and a beanbag chair. My record player and vinyl collection from college sat in the corner.

Nathalie's bedroom was nicely put together with a bed, colorful sheets, curtains, dresser, bookshelves and even a big mirror. My room, on the other hand, was a disaster. I had been sleeping on a leaky air mattress for the last month, and I had barely even unpacked my bags since returning from Israel. There was a film of dust on the floor and—a sign that I was writing again—the walls were cluttered with notes and sketches that I'd pinned up.

When it began to rain, we felt claustrophobic. I went to the kitchen to fix coffee. Soon the kettle was screaming, and I had the French Press primed. Joel came out of my room carrying the instruments. The thin drug dealer looked sickly in his oversized Red Hot Chili Peppers T-shirt. He sat down on the busted rocking chair and massaged his dimpled chin. Finally, he spoke.

"Your friend, Ari, visited me in jail," he said. "Bet you didn't know that."

I guess he'd been reading the notes on my wall. Ari's name was everywhere. This information, however, was a big surprise. I brought Joel his coffee. He shifted his body in the chair and took a few sips before telling me the rest.

"Ari was out west for some reason. He heard I was locked up in Minnesota for taking acid over state lines and decided he'd swing by and pay me a visit. I never figured out who told him. Maybe his brother, Jeremy?"

"How was the visit?" I asked.

"I refused to see him," Joel answered.

"I don't understand. Weren't you happy to see a friend?"

"Hell no. I didn't want anyone from home to see me like that. I told Ari to fuck off."

Joel's begrudged embarrassment made me laugh. I pictured Ari waltzing into the jail house and then getting slapped in the face by Joel's swinging moods.

"You guys were never best of pals anyway," I said, trying to sound sympathetic. I usually liked to hear what was on Joel's mind, but anything that had to do with Ari made me nervous. I picked up my guitar. Joel had changed the strings and tuned it nicely. I started playing a simple bum-ditty beat full of G's and C's to start us off until Joel took up the melody, plucking and sliding in a bluesy way. Suddenly, Joel muffled his instrument with his hand.

"Anyway," he announced. "I've decided to forgive Ari for coming to visit me. A few years have gone by now. What the hell? If you're friends with him, then I want to be friends too."

"How generous of you. Are you sure you're ready?" I said, maybe a bit too sarcastic.

"Stop it. Do you have his number? I want to call."

That's what I loved about Joel. Anything that couldn't be done immediately wasn't worth doing. We finished our coffee in big gulps. Then, as though we were schoolboys daring each other to call girls, we dialed Ari's number. When Joel became squeamish, I put the call on speaker-phone, forcing him to talk.

Ari answered laughing. "I was about to call you," he said. "Had the phone in my hand. You live on the West Side, right?"

"949 Columbus. At the corner of one hundred and sixth."

"Great. Mind if we stop by?"

"We?"

"Me and Hailey."

"Where are you?"

"The grocery. We've got stuff for brunch, but can't hail a cab in this rain. You're only a few blocks away."

"You'll share breakfast? Myles never has any food," Joel said, barging into the conversation.

"Who's that?" Ari asked.

"Surprise," I teased.

Ari said they would be by in ten. When we hung up, Joel looked at me and shrugged his shoulders. We improvised another song while we waited for the buzzer.

Enter Hailey: She stepped inside confidently. Her tight jeans were tucked into tall leather boots, and her frilly summer blouse exposed the freckled tops of her breasts. She was a bit chubbier than I had expected, but I immediately thought her well-suited for Ari. I took her umbrella, and she shook the rain out of her blonde hair. Hailey's motions were graceful, yet spontaneous. Her voice was cheery.

"You must be Myles," she said, giving me her hand. Ari was still in the hall, shaking off. When he came inside he put his arm around Hailey's waist.

"We brought groceries!" Hailey announced, leaping further into the apartment and out of Ari's grasp. She placed a large bag on the counter. A raisin challah was jutting out along with a bottle of cava. Then she found herself face-to-face with Joel.

"You must be the surprise?" Hailey said, holding out her hand. Ari squeezed past. He greeted Joel and introduced Hailey.

"Long time..." Joel said.

"Not since…" Ari answered. And that was as far as they got concerning Joel's planned apology.

Everyone was hungry, so Hailey and Joel set to work preparing brunch while I gave Ari a tour of the apartment. Finding my roommate's door locked, I explained how Nathalie had caught me sleeping in her bed whenever she was away. Then I showed Ari my room.

Ari wasn't surprised to learn I'd been mooching. He understood when he saw my deflated mattress and he was amused by all the notes climbing up the wall in my bedroom.

"I see you're still writing about us?" he asked, spying his name on a few of the scraps.

"Always. This time I'll make us famous," I promised, letting him read everything. I wasn't afraid what he'd think. I hadn't slandered, and there were no embarrassing confessions buried in the prose. Besides, I wanted Ari to be interested in my project.

"What's it called?" he asked.

"*Idle in September,*" I answered.

"Yes, yes, yes," Ari said. "Sounds great. Do you still write the same way—seeing the title and the last scene first?"

"So far this one is different. I'm not sure of anything yet. There's a music band on a road trip. The book takes place after 9/11."

Ari laughed when he noticed the blue-squishy ball we used to toss around during college study breaks, lying in the corner.

"You kept that?" he asked.

"The ball is blessed," I said. "Whenever I unpack in a new city, somehow it always turns up."

A few throws landed us back in the living room. Hailey was frying onions and mushrooms for omelets, the kettle was screaming again, and Joel had sliced up the challah.

"Are you any good?" Hailey asked about my guitar.

"Not really. Besides a few lessons, I'm self-taught."

"Can you play for the kids in my class? Their music teacher is on maternity leave, and I don't sing. We're desperate for music."

I shot a glance toward Ari, hoping to get his approval, but he was in the corner with Joel, choosing a record.

"Please come! The children will love you," Hailey insisted.

Joel and Ari finally decided on a Grateful Dead album. The wandering tune didn't let me off the hook.

"Sure, why not?" I offered, hardly sounding committed.

There was no table to set, so we arranged everything on the floor and distributed plates. Ari sat close to Hailey, I took the beanbag chair, and Joel sat above us on a stool.

"This is very Bohemian, Myles," Hailey observed as we all took first bites. Then Ari started talking business.

"You missed our meeting last week," he accused. "You promised you'd come."

"What meeting?" I answered.

Hailey laughed. "I told you he wouldn't remember," she said, playfully slapping Ari's knee. "Ari came home sloppy after that little party you guys threw on the Fourth," she continued, slurring her voice to mock her boyfriend's drunken behavior. "All he could talk about was how Myles said he'd come to a meeting."

"That's not true," Ari protested.

Hailey overruled him. "Yes it is," she said. "And you were still going on about it in the morning. Remember? I asked you if Myles was as drunk as you were at the party. You said he was in such poor shape he had to go home early. Then I suggested that if you really want Myles to come to your meeting, you better call and remind him. Too bad you never listen to me."

"Fine," Ari conceded. "I should have called. But Myles, let's be serious for a minute. I spoke to Professor Murphy. He wants to meet you. He says he has a job for you."

"A job? But I'm already employed."

"This will pay a lot better than what you're making at that restaurant. I promise."

"What does he have in mind?"

"Meet with him. He'll explain."

"I don't know. Did he say when?"

"Come tomorrow. There's a meeting in the evening so we'll all be there early to set up. You can stay for the after party, too."

"What time?"

"Come at six. Murphy will want to talk to you in private. Then I can show you around. People usually start rolling in around seven, after they get off work. We order food and plan for upcoming anti-war rallies. You'll learn a lot about what's going on in Iraq and Afghanistan from the veterans."

I looked at Hailey. "What do you make of this group?" I asked her.

"Not all my type, but they're nice," she said. "Ari has a great relationship with his professor and Murphy is an amazing speaker. But the wars are awful, and the veterans all have such sad stories. You feel kind of helpless. They are definitely a unique bunch though. They collect all kinds of gadgets, and it's a cool apartment. Once, we burned incense and meditated together. I liked that a lot."

"Really? You meditated?" Joel immediately got curious about the spiritual aspect.

"Well, some of us did. Some of the people in the group still need to loosen up."

When the rain finally stopped, Joel popped the bottle of Cava that Ari and Hailey had brought. We made mimosas and went upstairs to the roof. Outside, the humidity had passed, and there was even a cool breeze. Joel and Ari played catch while I pointed out landmarks to Hailey. I showed her the *Stranger's Gate* where I always entered Central Park, *Duke Ellington Boulevard* and Columbia University in the background. I didn't stop there. I started naming characters I had imagined and described their role in my book about Ari. Hailey was impressed.

"Wow," she said, lighting a cigarette. "I can tell it's real for you." Then she made me promise again that I'd play music for the children at the preschool where she taught. "I think you'd be great," she insisted.

A patch of clouds passed over the sun, darkening the sky again. We all sat down on the ledge and dangled our legs over the roof. The humidity was returning, and our drinks had lost their fizz. Ari got rather showy about kissing Hailey in front of us. Watching them, I understood right away why he loved her. Hailey had a great, echoing laugh. When she blushed, her entire complexion warmed.

I know lonely Joel was disgusted to see anyone happy with a girl, but I was all in favor of Ari and Hailey's affections and glad they'd come over. Later, when they packed up to go, I was hoping that Joel would leave with them. I was tired of having company, and I wanted some time alone to work on the book. Joel, of course, looked determined to stay and chat. He had already taken out his little bag of pot and wouldn't stop rolling a joint, not even to say goodbye to Ari and Hailey.

Not long after they'd gone downstairs, I heard Ari shouting up to me from the street. I ran to the window and threw it open. Ari stood on the sidewalk holding the blue ball in his hand.

"So you don't forget tomorrow!" he yelled, tossing the ball up to me. I caught the ball on the second throw and turned it around until I found where Ari had scribbled the address on the rubber. Then I gave him a thumbs-up and closed the window. When I turned around, Joel was waiting for me with the joint in his mouth. He sat in the rocking chair, scowling.

"Come on," I said. "Not in here. Let's go back upstairs."

"You have no idea how bored I was," Joel said, lighting his work. "I still really hate that guy."

9:00 P.M., Wednesday, March 5, 2008

How long does a cigarette last? All I could do was count the seconds. Hailey lingered in the hall, burning half-a-dozen while I struggled through a craving. At last, she left. I stood up and stretched. I was sweating buckets under my arms. Lee and I lit cigarettes. The smoke burned my eyes and nostrils. Lee coughed and hacked. Then he sat down on the couch, buried his head in his hands and began mumbling broken phrases.

Suddenly, I felt the urge to run after Hailey. I slipped on my loafers, tucked that Luger into my pants, and flew out the door. Lee yelled after me. I didn't reply. The stubs of Hailey's cigarettes were piled on the floor near the banister. Outside, the misty street glimmered. I let myself believe that I was hot on Hailey's trail, racing down 75th street until I hit Park Avenue. I peered down all the cross-streets in search of her blonde hair. Nothing. My chase was hopeless. She was gone, vanished in the fog.

Never mind. I was glad I'd acted on instinct and gotten out of that apartment. The fresh air helped clear my head.

I checked my phone. Nathalie's texts were venomous. She described herself in different costumes. She had opened a bottle of wine. When she touched herself, she said her skin tingled as though sunburned.

Should I give up this nonsense and go to her? On the corner of 75th and Third, I stuck out my hand for a taxi. A car pulled up, but I couldn't bring myself to get inside. If I left the East Side, I'd be abandoning Ari. This time, I refused to run away.

Locks and Keys
(Late July 2007)

The day of my meeting with Murphy, I made a point of locking myself out as I left the apartment. What the hell. I couldn't think of a better way to show Nathalie I missed her. I hadn't seen my roommate in over a week. By now I was a little worried about her, but I needed an excuse to call her up. Damn that actress. We were always playing games. This endless, "Where did you sleep last night?" routine lit wildfire jealousies. We'd lock each other out, and only open the door again when the sexual tension was boiling. This was never convenient and always got out of hand. No matter how ruthlessly we toyed with each other, however, we'd still wind up sleeping together at least half the month.

Musing about the female protagonist I'd cast in my novel about Ari, a character named Beth, I found myself jotting down a poem in the shape of a woman's hourglass:

Impulsive Monday:
Their minds threaded through the knot of not,
None be-wedded to the thought of "us;"
Preferred scenes of life to love,
Cruel orgasms at leisure.
They roomed together
Forgot to lunch,
Fought twice
A week
Fucked
Once a month.
Hearts stranded
Sundays without a touch.
Lonely strangers collecting lust.

God. Poetry. I hated that rot.

A black and brown striped cat roamed my neighborhood. He was welcome in the bodegas nearby, and always gave purring company to the Blacks and Latinos sitting outside their tenements, betting on chess games. I called the poor cat "Duke Ellington" on account of the nicknamed jazz boulevard—106th street—that he liked to stalk. But Duke was a lousy companion. He distrusted me. Even when I brought him scraps of food, he'd never come closer than a yard before he'd turn and run, his lime green eyes filled with judgment.

When I rounded the corner of my building, I encountered Duke in the alley, licking his paws. The spying cat followed me as far as Central Park. That last look he gave me as I climbed the stone steps to the Strangers' Gate, that contemptuous snicker he seemed to utter, made me feel cursed.

The morning's mocking poetics, characters, and nature all faded fast as I fell into the routine of work. Another slow day at the restaurant. Between seating couples and hung-over gossip-girls, all I could do was plot my affair with Nathalie. I wanted to spend the weekend with her and finally show her a good time. As long as Ari wasn't shitting me about the job with Murphy, I could count on some extra money. A full week of work meant I could blow everything I made on the weekend.

Suddenly, I was starving for sex. I thought of Nathalie's cycle. There was a full moon coming, and Nathalie was always crazy when the moon came out. I thought we could go up on the roof again and spread out some blankets and cushions. Always performing, she never cared if people saw us. She'd want me to go hard on her, pin her down, dabble my tongue between her legs.

On a break, I called her up.

"What do *you* want?" Nathalie said. She was bad at acting sassy.

"Don't bite. I'm only wondering if you'll be by the apartment tonight?"

"Wouldn't *you* like to know?"

"I would. I'm locked out."

"You're not serious."

"Nat, I left the keys in the basket. You've done that too."

"Do you have any idea where I am right now? How far out of my way that is?"

"You haven't been home in a week. How could I have any clue where you are? I'm only calling to say that if you happen to be in the city tonight, I'd appreciate it if you could stop by and let me in."

"I'll call you back."

"No, wait, Nat. I'm at work. I'll miss the call. Tell me now: Can you come? Yes or no?"

She put me on hold for a minute to make me sweat. Then she returned.

"Fine," she sighed. "I'll be there."

"Great. Thanks, Nathalie. What time should I meet you?"

"Late."

"Do you have a performance tonight?"

"None of your business. Look, meet me at nine."

"Will you have a drink with me?"

"Wrong question," she said. I heard the phone click.

I laughed. 9PM meant she wanted me to buy her dinner and yes, a fuck. She was using me, but I didn't care. Actually I was relieved. I now had the perfect exit strategy if the meeting with Ari's professor dragged on too long.

I went back to my shift feeling pretty sly, but work quickly numbed my buzz. I blamed it all on the music. *Imagine.* They played that John Lennon song top of every hour and the phony peace-poet's verses got stuck in my head.

To pass the time I tried daydreaming more about Nathalie, but now I was dreading meeting Murphy. I thought something was strange about the set-up, and I was sure there was a catch. With a recession on the horizon, not many people were giving away jobs in New York.

After work, I set out for Murphy's, dribbling the blue ball on which Ari had written his professor's address. I took my time getting there. Madison, Park, Lexington, Third, Second, First. The late afternoon sun cast orange, slow moving shadows. I followed 75th Street past York Avenue—a dead end blocked by the FDR expressway. Thick steam billowed out of a Con-Ed plant's brick smokestack. A red awning opposite marked Murphy's building.

I rang the bell and the door clicked open. Piano music filled the stairwell with the bright melody of a Jelly Roll Rag.

Whoever was playing, however, couldn't keep the tempo even and often made mistakes. On the second floor, I paused to eavesdrop. Male voices were joking around. I knocked on the big red door and was surprised how quickly everyone quieted.

The door swung open. I was pulled inside. The lights went out. All I could see were the ends of cigarettes flashing about. Smoke burned my eyes until they'd tied a blindfold. I tried to squirm free, tried to scream, but a large hand muffled my mouth.

"Who are you?" my attackers shouted. "Who sent you?" I was restrained in a strongman's grip and shoved into a couch.

"Ari!" I yelled, gasping for air. "Murphy invited—"

Down the hall, the piano music resumed. Then I heard Ari laughing. They turned on the lights and freed me. I was dizzy and drenched in sweat.

"Myles, meet Landon," Ari grinned, introducing the black brute who had straitjacketed me. Landon was grotesque. Pink, shrapnel scars streaked his cheek and forehead. "You already know Chris," Ari said, nodding toward his other accomplice.

The two men offered me handshakes that hurt my wrist. Then they wandered off to other corners of the apartment where they resumed different private projects. Chris was drawing in his sketchbook. Landon was tinkering with an old computer. A documentary about 9/11 was playing on the television.

"What the hell, Ari? You scared the shit out of me!" I said, wiping my face on my sleeve.

Ari was enjoying his little joke. "Been a while since I pulled one on you," he said. Then he helped me up and ushered me into another room.

The space was modest and square with two windows. There was a coffee table wedged between a foldable cot, and a sofa. A steel wire grate guarded the ornate fireplace. Ari wasted no time fixing me a drink. He handed me a glass that rattled with ice and smelled like flat soda.

"What is this place?" I demanded, shyly sipping the whiskey and Coke. Ari shrugged. He said they had recently moved headquarters, hence the lack of decorations. Professor Murphy would explain the rest.

"Where's Murphy?" I asked.

"Giving Lee a piano lesson."

I waited for Ari to change the subject.

"Alright, spill it," he finally said, sounding nervous. He was dying to know what I thought of Hailey.

"She's great. Sexy, smart. You hit the jackpot," I answered.

"Do you think she's a bit trashy?"

"Because she's blonde and smokes?"

"Yes, yes, yes."

"You know I like trashy girls, they're kinks."

Next thing I knew, Ari was confiding in me. He thought a significant change had taken place in his life. "It's been a good summer," he said. "I've got security now. I'm not so easily rattled."

"And Hailey?" I asked, "How does she fit in?"

"Look. I'm not going to marry her tomorrow if that's what you're asking."

"Does she want to get married?"

"Wants to? Yes. She's twenty-eight. She wants to get married—sometime."

"Is that a problem?"

Ari shook his head. "All that matters right now is that we get along and that she supports my work here. We're having fun, and I trust her. Hey, did I ever tell you what I said to her when I asked her out?"

I shook my head.

"That was last summer. I said, 'I think we ought to see if we don't fall in love.' I've never been so forward with a girl."

I was about to make fun of his romanticism, but we were interrupted by the sound of the heavy piano rolling down the hallway.

"Would you look at that? Quite an audience gathered for you, young Lee," Professor Murphy said, his sharp Irish accent echoing. The men who had participated in Ari's prank a half hour earlier reacted with obedience. They dropped what they were doing and stood up straight with military attention.

Murphy saw me standing with Ari. He motioned for me to follow him to his office. "I don't suppose you lads could lend a hand?" he asked his audience before ushering me down the hall. "'Tis time to decorate. Be right at home. Lee says he wants the piano in the other room. Can't say I see a reason not to. Please: Do feel free. Redecorate all you like. 'Tis good to keep the energy flowing. Change things up from time to time like a storm in the atmosphere. You can even draw on the walls if you like. Let's have some bloody free expression!"

Inside Murphy's office, volumes of books towered above me. The shelves were on the verge of caving in. So many titles, my eyes didn't know where to look.

"Ari told me you're a writer. "Where, then, do you find your philosophy?" Murphy asked.

"Philosophy? I'm not sure I have any. Life moves faster than reason, and I live by my whims," I said, kneeling down to view a lower shelf stocked with books in German.

"Could you bear Kant?"

"A little. What's this?" I said, eying Murphy's swastika labeled copy of *Mein Kampf.*

"History would have been very different had the German people actually read that book. They'd have seen what a madman Hitler was."

Murphy's shadow drifted over me. I pushed Hitler's tome back in its place.

"Marquis de Sade?" he pressed. "There's another fine devil, no doubt?"

"Yes, but his philosophy is incomplete."

"Fair enough."

Now Murphy wore the distinguished smile of a man who knew he had impressed someone. The rest came rapid fire.

"Rousseau?" he asked.

"A lovely child."

"Joyce?"

"As real as it gets. He's the expert at suggestion."

"Henry Miller?"

"The best sex I ever read. He kicks all the romance out of being an expat."

"Ayn Rand?"

I made a face that finally stopped him. Then the old man laughed his scratchy laugh and begged I sit down in the leather chair before his desk. I obeyed, watching him slowly settle into his seat across from me. From his desk drawer, Murphy produced a pair of reading glasses, a yellow legal pad, and a folder. He arranged these things meticulously, then looked me top to bottom, his eyes black as olives and his dagger-tongue still twisting every word he spoke.

"Mr. Fletcher, if you don't mind, I'll be asking you some questions. Then we'll see what you can do for us."

His tone made me a little angry with Ari. I wasn't expecting to be interviewed. I'd understood that the job was as good as mine. All I needed to do was show up. Grudgingly, I nodded acceptance of our conditional meeting. Murphy adjusted his square spectacles and stared back and forth between his notes and me. Somehow, his bony hands and knuckles never stopped crackling with tension. He had smoker's breath, and when he smiled, he revealed jagged, yellow teeth.

"Tell me, Myles. How does a lad like you see the present?" he asked.

"You mean in the context of my writing?"

Murphy nodded.

"I don't," I answered. "The present sees me."

"You mean to say you haven't any control over what you type. You'll be one of those stream of consciousness writers, no doubt?"

"Don't try to put me in a box," I protested.

Murphy rephrased his prompt. "Let's try something, shall we? Do you know Big Echo?"

I shook my head.

"One of Ari's games. You know, a bit of therapy for the boys. Our members like to play. Here's how it works. I'll choose a subject, you'll speak spontaneously. Shall we give it a try?"

For about an hour, I was asked to give spontaneous monologues, elaborating on my every opinion until each prompt became ridiculous. Murphy employed a long-winded method of interrogation. He was keen to provoke me, wanted to draw me out, speaking perhaps too honestly about personal subjects until I was lost in the flood of my words. Then he would change course abruptly, responding to something buried in my speech with yet another pointed question.

At times, we were very literary. Murphy wanted to know about my fiction, and he was curious why I detested poetry.

"I can't take poets seriously," I argued. "Most of what I've read amounts to obscure, self-absorbed rants. Poetry and philosophy ought to be tools for getting at the spokes of words. Not an excuse to ramble about post-modern emotions."

I worried that I bored Murphy with my various theories. Especially when he began scratching away on a piece of paper some cryptic slogan in Gaelic: "Tiocfaidh ár l´a." After a while, I thought my efforts were hopeless. The old man had no intention of hiring me. Strangely, the more he tested me with questions, the more eager I was to please him. I wanted to get the job on my merits, and I would say anything to show I was worthy.

"What are you writing?" I had to know about the Gaelic.

"You ought to remember," Murphy laughed. "We've met before, you know? Ari took you to hear me lecture. I spoke on the history of the Irish Republican Army. You fell asleep. No matter. `Tis true. Ask Ari. I don't mind that you fell asleep either. Though, `tis a bit of a wonder to me how you ever managed. You sat not three rows from the front, and I've a reputation for rising to the sound of me own voice."

Was the old man joking? He didn't wait for me to laugh. "Never mind," Murphy said, smiling his awful smile. "Let's resume. I'd like to know what you thought of Cornell: That campus, those students, and your professors. I've a sense you were…uncomfortable there."

"Uncomfortable? No. I'd say restrained maybe. I grew up in Ithaca. I was too close to home."

"What about your father? He was being investigated during your studies, wasn't he?"

"I'd rather not talk about my father."

"Very well. But being near your parents and your friend's family did make you claustrophobic. Did it not?"

"Ari's father and my dad were colleagues. They're both doctors. Ithaca is a small town. When my father messed up, the news was everywhere."

"I understand. Tell me, how did you find the students at Cornell. What was your view of them?"

"Most were boring. That was the 90's. All anyone wanted to do was make money."

"Oh yes: 'our day will come.' That's the slogan you asked about, by the way. 'Tiocfaidh ár l´a.' `Tis a prayer for a united Ireland, but I suppose the phrase suits capitalists and communists alike. Were you with the socialists at the university?"

"You're asking: Was I a member?"

"Yes, exactly. Membership is a fair measure of one's loyalty and commitment."

"No. That's going too far. I was never a member of any party. I was only curious about their meetings. The socialists threw good parties. I enjoyed their eccentricities. They were always playing pranks and fighting the administration. But then their rhetoric got out of hand."

"Rhetoric. I sense you find that element of politics disturbing. You despise choosing sides. Perhaps you don't believe in sentiment, principles and reason?"

He was wearing me down. I didn't like how he summed up my character at every turn.

"The job?" I asked, finally cutting him off. Murphy leaned back in his chair, caressing his grizzly chin.

"Yes, work will set you free, won't it? Myles, tell me your politics and opinion of the wars, then I'll know if you can help."

"I have no allegiance or political opinions. Honestly, I'm only here because of Ari."

"Right, Ari. So you've tracked your old friend down. Now to make amends."

"What do you know about that?"

"I suppose I know everything."

"You couldn't."

"But I'm sure I do. I make it me business to know everything about anyone who enters me house. Wouldn't you do the same? Myles, I notice you're quite tense. Are you thirsty? Perhaps another drink?

About time he offered, I was parched.

Murphy opened a drawer underneath his desk, brought out a bottle of Jameson and opened the folder he had on his desk. He sighed when he saw my glass.

"Drat, I haven't any ice. Wait a moment?" he said, taking my glass and standing up to go to the kitchen. He brought the folder with him. Upon returning with the drinks, he read from my dossier:

"Cornell. Class of 2000. New York. You went cross-country with Ari and Dylan after. Then you returned to the city. About a year later you had your falling out over the lass. Melissa. Was that her name? Off to Israel next. Was it a Zionist's retreat? No. I think not. A girl stole your heart in Tel Aviv, but you've left her too. You were only entertaining yourself for a time. Unfinished business Stateside kept you from marrying. Is that not all true?"

I guess I'd made a face. Murphy stopped reading and watched me closely.

"Speak up, Myles," he said. "Correct me if I'm wrong."

I shrugged, disappointing him.

"Well, I won't force you. Besides, home you've come and that's what matters. I'll let bygones be," Murphy relented. "The rest is easy. You've been living on the West Side, and you've been busy. You've published several stories about your friend, Ari. I have them here," he said, waving one of the clippings. "You've a flair for memoir, I see. And, yes, that about sums up. Now you've come to me, looking for work."

"Ari told you all that?"

"No. I found it all me-self. It wasn't hard. A man leaves a reckless trail when he writes. Myles, I'll tell you plainly, I am interested in the goings-on between you and Ari. He's a good pupil of mine, and he's done fine work for our little movement. But I worry sometimes that he needs watching and some rowdy encouragement. Then he might better enjoy life. We mustn't neglect ourselves, shall we? All work and no play makes Jack a dull boy. I like that about you. You seem to bring out some of the charm lost on our Ari. You're a good friend to him."

"I'm not friendly—"

"You are. What happened between you two is long in the past and ought to be forgotten."

"I'm not sure I can."

"You *can*, and you *will*, if you want to work here."

Suddenly, Murphy stood up. "Myles, I'll make this plain and simple," he said, pacing in front of me. "Our dear friend, Ari, could use a shepherd, but truth is I want someone to help keep track of all me lonely boys. That's where me interest in you begins. We need to document everything. You'll be our secretary, take notes on our meetings and act as confidant to the boys when I'm not here. I can't be their only advisor, after all. Besides, you're their age. 'Tis more appropriate. I imagine this will challenge you at first, but I know you'll get through to them in time. We're engaged in a political mission. Me boys are veterans. They are ex-pats, and they are patriots. They all hate this war. They hate the government for hosting elections whilst the populous is distracted by the economy. You must understand, the wars are the central issue in 2008, not our big banks and petty commerce. You'll find me boys quite troubled. They've seen hell during their time of service, and they're desperate to talk. I'll pay you to meet with them separate and collect their stories. Will that suit you?"

Before I could answer, Murphy tossed me two copies of the colorful underground pamphlets that the group published. I was startled by their titles—"Memoirs of Torture" and "Roadside Rebels."

"Why do you say Ari needs watching?" I backtracked. I couldn't understand why it was urgent I join the ranks.

"Are you worried about your friend?" Murphy flipped my question.

"Should I be?"

"You *are* worried about him. You must be or else you'd not have come."

"Ari invited me."

"Myles, I'll tell you something about Ari. While you were away on your travels, he was off touring the country. He saw an awful lot on that trip—the poverty, the injustices of capitalism, the utter neglect. What a bloody mess we've gotten ourselves into in this country. Ari experienced this depravity alone before he sought me out. You mustn't discount his compassion. I'd say your friend has a poet's soul, but then you'd mock him. Wouldn't you, Myles? No, you underestimate Ari. He hasn't the voice to speak his mind. He never has. He's been damned, as you say, to obscurity. But I reckon he'd be a leader if he had your pen behind him."

Murphy saw my distrust, if not my confusion. He knew he needed to simplify the contract.

"You see, Myles," he said, pointing to one of the pamphlets. "Ari and every one of me boys here be noble souls bearing noble dreams, but without a skilled pen behind them they haven't got a voice. Write for them. That's all I'm asking."

"You make it sound quite mercenary," I said, still looking for a better explanation.

"Well, you *are* entitled to care," Murphy stabbed back. "The job is simple. I'm asking you to spell out our member's thoughts. You won't have to think a thing on your own. Just draw the dialogue together so that it makes some good sense and fills the page."

"What's my pay?" I asked, knowing I'd take the gig no matter what Murphy offered.

"Is it worth five hundred a week to you?"

"Can you do six?"

"No."

"Five-fifty?"

"No."

"Under the table?"

"Uncle Sam will never know."

"Deal," I said. "Five is plenty."

9:30 P.M., Wednesday, March 5, 2008

I started back to the apartment, walking slowly at first and still debating my decision not to flee. When I heard footsteps behind me, I picked up the pace. I looked back. Nobody was there. I stuck to First Avenue and started running. I was certain someone was following. At the corner of 75th and First, Chris leapt out. Grabbing my arm, he covered my mouth and dragged me into the nearest nook. I knew better than to scream. Chris could snap my neck with ease.

"Somebody flew the coop," he said, slowly letting me go.

"Was that necessary?" I asked.

"I didn't want to call your name in case Murphy's following me."

"Why would Murphy—" I started to say. Then I realized how disheveled Chris looked. Something had happened to him downtown.

"What are you doing here?" I asked. "Aren't you supposed to be in Times Square?"

"I never got off the subway," he explained.

"Weren't you with the others?"

"No. I was with Landon in the beginning, but he got off a stop early. I needed more time to think everything through, so I took the train to Brooklyn. Then I turned back. I was going to get off at Times Square. Honest. I still had time. I could have joined them. But something stopped me. So I rode up here. When I got outside, I saw you trying to hail a cab."

"Come with me back to the apartment?" I suggested.

"No. Let's go someplace public. That's safer."

"CitiBar is across the street," I said, pointing to the neon sign.

Chris led the way. The pub was quiet. Two men were playing pool, another sat at the bar, watching a basketball game. We found a table near the stage, the same place where we had first met. One of Chris's drawings was still hanging on the wall.

"What's going on back at the apartment?" Chris asked.

"Lee's there. He couldn't go through with the plan either."

"Why were you outside?"

"Ari's girlfriend, Hailey, came by. I made a mistake. I regretted not letting her in, so I ran after her."

"Any luck catching her?"

"No. She must have hailed a cab. Come on, Chris, what are we doing here? Lee's waiting all alone. The kid's a mess. Besides, the attack could start any minute. We should be at the apartment."

"I need a drink," Chris said.

"Do you have money?" I asked.

Chris stood up and went to the bar. He brought back two pints of Guinness.

"Don't you find it a little strange that an Irishman is leading our group?" he asked, taking a long, first sip.

"Now you think of this?"

"Don't get smart."

I gulped my drink. The foam caught in my throat. Someone put a dollar in the jukebox. A series of Lou Reed songs played. I wondered what Chris would have to say about the music now, but was nervous to ask. When I stared past him at the basketball game that was on TV, Chris gave me a little slap on the cheek, demanding my attention.

"Myles, cut that out," he snapped. "I'm trying to tell you something. Can I trust you?"

After Hours
(Late July 2007)

The scene had changed during the hour I was in Professor Murphy's office, interviewing for the secretarial position. The boys unpacked decorations, dimmed the lights, ordered pizzas, and brought up cases of beer. When I re-emerged, everyone was drinking. Music blared, cigarette smoke clouded the room, and there were girls there. I had to get cross-town to meet Nathalie, but nobody would let me leave. By the time I fled the party, not even the fastest taxi in New York could save me from being late.

I met Frida in the kitchen. The girl was hardly attractive. She had red hair and her big nose was pierced with a hoop. Fluorescent Livestrong bracelets advocating every hopeful cause lined her freckled wrists, and she wore a vintage Boy-Scout uniform she'd found at Goodwill.

"You're Ari's friend?" she asked, giving me her hand. "I'm an illustrator for Murphy's underground magazine. Chris and I do the cover art."

The music was too loud. I couldn't hear. Frida laughed, aware of my discomfort. "You'll get used to their music," she promised. Just don't tell any of the veterans you can't take the volume. They live by Metal. That's what got them through their service."

"Through what?" I yelled.

"The war! They start listening during basic training," Frida shouted back over the crashing noise and wailing vocals. "The army plays new recruits videos loaded with heavy metal music and body building themes. That gets their adrenaline pumping and turns them into mean, green, fighting machines." She gave me a playful nudge with her ass and got close to my ear. "They've got their playlist going now. That's holy. But later you can pick an album or go on Youtube. Ask Landon if there's something you want to hear. He's the DJ."

I watched Landon scroll through songs on his smart phone, compiling a playlist for the party. His scars bulged as he drank. When he saw me staring, I quickly looked away and asked for the bathroom. Frida pointed down the hall. She and Dylan were making out on the couch when I returned.

Now I took in the rest of the apartment. A string of Christmas lights illuminated the brick walls. A tall palm tree cast spiky shadows in the corner. Near the sofa, Alan was talking to that obnoxious lawyer, Sam. Landon, Chris and Lee, meanwhile, were scribbling with pastels on the wall. In the other room, the TV, computer and piano had all been moved to the side to make room for a podium. Suddenly, Ari banged a gavel and everyone quieted down.

"Boys and girls, gather around. A moment please," Professor Murphy said, putting his hand on my shoulder and leading me to the podium. "This, here, is Myles Fletcher. Friend of Ari's and friend of ours. He's a writer and a good one at that. I've asked him to copy down your stories and incorporate them into our magazine. Don't be shy. I trust you will all introduce yourselves and share your experiences."

There were calls for a longer speech, but Murphy was eager to see the mural being drawn on the center room's wall. Realizing the hour, I started toward the door, but Ari stood in my way.

"Where are you going?" he asked.

"I have to meet my roommate."

"You should stay. Meet some more of the members."

"I'll be here all next week. Can't I meet them then?"

Ari took me by the arm and dragged me back to the party. In front of the door to the other room, Alan and Rachel were coloring on the wall. They handed me a crayon, and I was expected to make my mark.

"Draw an elephant!" "Draw the President!" "Draw Cheney bird hunting!" The excited crowd demanded political caricatures from the inspired artists.

I decided to draw my feet walking up the wall, kicked off my sandals and asked Rachel for help. Next thing I knew, Chris and Landon lifted me up so that I could walk the wall while Rachel traced around my bare toes. When they let me down, I was glad to take a hit from a passing joint. As soon as I was high, the colors became more vibrant.

"This is fun," I told Ari, adding that I'd stay a little longer. Pleased, Ari took me aside.

"I just got off the phone with my brother," he said, fixing us another one of those toxic cocktails. "You remember Jeremy? He's coming to visit."

"He's staying with you?"

"Of course. Cheers, Myles. Here's to your new job and to ending the wars."

With that, Ari set me loose again. By the piano, I tried asking Ethan about Iraq, but he was hardly interested in talking to me. He'd brought his girlfriend, Josie—the small, freckle-faced blonde he'd been with since high school—to the party. He kept looking around, drained his glass impatiently and wouldn't stop staring at Josie, especially when she talked to other men. He was feeling lonely, but I couldn't take his jealousy seriously. I could read Josie's lips. Every sentence she spoke began with "Ethan."

"I suppose he'll make me talk to you," Ethan grumbled, nodding his head toward Professor Murphy.

"Nobody is *making* you do anything."

"I'll tell you my story. But not here. Let's talk in private."

We made vague plans to meet. Then Ethan went out to the fire escape for a cigarette. I was on my way out when I bumped into Dylan again.

"Where are you going?" he asked. He'd carried a case of beer up from the basement. The grin on his face indicated he'd seen action. I followed him into the kitchen.

"Your shirt is off a button," I said, pointing out his sloppy clean-up job after his frisk in the cellar with Frida. Dylan quickly undid the buttons and straightened his collar.

"She's a wild cat," he said, explaining Frida's nymphomania. "It won't last."

Then he changed the subject. "Why the hell didn't we go to New Orleans?" he asked, growing nostalgic for our time on the road together. He was all the time running a finger through his hair until the wavy blonde strands stood on edge. "I'm jealous, Myles. You and Ari kept traveling, but I got stuck in New York."

I filled Dylan in as best I could, leaving out the parts about Melissa. I would have liked to talk to him longer, maybe even go somewhere else for a drink, but then my phone rang. Nathalie would never forgive me unless I left immediately.

Dylan understood. We made plans to meet, and shook hands. Then he gave me a beer for the road. I was in a cab before I realized I'd forgotten to say goodbye to Ari.

9:35 P.M., Wednesday, March 5, 2008

What Chris had to tell me was pure speculation. During his long subway ride, he'd developed a raw conspiracy theory. Now, he wanted to convince me.

"Did you know Murphy flew me to Ireland last year?"

I shook my head.

"That's right. You wouldn't. That was before you joined. Murphy flew me over to run an errand."

"Didn't you ask questions?"

"Who was I to refuse a free trip? Besides, I wanted to see the murals in Belfast," Chris said, explaining how the Irish city is famous for the political art that came out of "The Troubles."

Murphy had suggested Chris use the chance to study their style, but the experiment was a disaster. "Next thing I know I'm handing over money-stuffed envelopes in a smoky bar," he recalled. "Murphy's pimple-faced Danny-boy held a gun under the table while his strongman counted the cash."

"Come on Chris, that was no secret. We all know Murphy's sentiments. He never lied about his role in the IRA."

"Sentiments? What about loyalties? Where does he get the money, Myles? Who is he manipulating Stateside in order to help his countrymen over there?"

"You'd know better than me."

"The IRA started disarming almost ten years ago. Did it ever occur to you that he could be part of a splinter group? Maybe his cronies sent him over here to start organizing for another round of terrorism."

"That still doesn't explain what he's doing here with us. If Murphy's working for the Irish, why would he care about American veterans and stopping the war?"

"Alright. Maybe he does believe in our cause. Maybe he is a true benefactor. More likely it's a ploy to get access to American banks. Think: Who's really supplying the money for all this?"

"Jim?"

"Of course it's Jim. He knows every banker in town. Once Murphy had him in his pocket he could afford all the guns he wanted, pay us off to create a distraction and then siphon money at his pleasure to feed IRA hacks."

"That's pretty imaginative, Chris. I don't know."

"Fine, consider this: After 9/11, everything tightened up, right? Security increased everywhere. That's why the IRA had to disarm so quickly. They didn't want to be grouped with the Arabs and be labeled terrorists. There's too much money at stake. The Irish don't want their accounts frozen by the CIA. They're nothing like Al Qaeda, but the Patriot Act lets the government play dirty with terrorists. Therefore, it was more profitable to make peace. Only hardliners like Murphy don't care. For them, peace is only downtime. They use it to plot their next big attack."

"That still doesn't explain tonight. Why our mission? Why the crazy death pact? If Murphy's that well-connected and he already has the money and guns he needs to satisfy his mission, he'd leave already. Why make us pledge our lives and carry out this operation in Times Square?"

"He doesn't want to leave a trail. If he kills us all, there won't be any witnesses."

"Stop that, Chris. Murphy's not going to kill anyone."

Chris was frustrated when I didn't accept his answer, or his theory. He held his heavy head in his hands, exhausted. "I don't know," he sighed, rubbing under his eyes. "I'm going mad. Nothing makes sense about tonight."

I finished my drink. "We should get back," I told Chris. "It's almost ten. Something might have happened by now."

"No way am I going to that apartment. You're sitting ducks."

"Where will you go?"

"Back downtown. I have to try and stop them. Come on, you know this doesn't feel right. We're being used."

"You don't believe blowing up the recruitment center will accomplish anything?" I asked.

"Not so loud."

"Sorry. Well, do you?"

"Of course I believe in the cause. We all do. And maybe the war debate will change when we take action. But what if we fail? What if Murphy abandons us?"

"That's a lot of ifs," I said, shrugging my shoulders.

Chris stood up. As he put his coat back on, I saw his belt. He was armed to the teeth with grenades, ammunition clips and a pistol.

"Here's the plan," Chris offered. "Get Lee and catch a cab. I'll text you where to meet me outside Penn Station."

My phone buzzed with a message as we shook hands. Nathalie was nervous. She asked what was holding me up.

I started writing my reply. By the time I looked up again, Chris had disappeared.

My Wicked Witch to the West
(Late July 2007)

Nathalie was sitting on our doorstep. First she refused to look at me, then she stood up and threw the door open. "Something's waiting for you upstairs," she warned as we climbed the stairs. "Would it kill you to clean up after yourself?"

She was dressed like a New Yorker. Stunning liberty—the length of her skirt, the frills around her shoulders, the lace on her blouse. She wouldn't discuss anything with me until I took care of the dead mouse she'd found in the kitchen.

"I'm so sick of this," she complained while I extracted the carcass from the blood-stained trap. "There must be a better way to keep the mice out."

"Why do you care? You're never here," I said.

Nathalie threw up her arms and stomped toward the door.

"Come on, Nat, I didn't mean that. Where are you going? Stay. Let's have a drink."

She rifled through her purse. "I'm going to the store," she said, letting out a furious sigh.

"What for?"

"You're exhausting, Myles. We need more mouse traps."

I followed her out. At first we struggled to talk while we shopped, but then we had fun in the back of the store. Everything Nat wanted to see was out of her reach, so I found a ladder.

"You want this one?" I offered.

"No, that one."

"Are you sure? These are glue traps. The mouse gets stuck and dies a slow death. Sounds pretty cruel."

"Stop it. Let me see."

I pulled Nathalie up on the ladder with me and made her kiss me. Her lips were dry, but the kiss was good. We crossed tongues, and I breathed in her carnation scent. We started laughing. But this was only an interlude. I knew the big fight would come soon enough.

Outside the store, I tempted Nathalie with my good news about the job with Murphy.

"Come on, Nat, let me take you out. I've got a surprise."

"The last time I let you take me out it was 4:30 in the morning when we got home. I had work at seven, and I was dead the whole next day. Besides, I can't stay at the apartment tonight."

"Why not?"

She made me wait while she checked her phone. Then she shrugged her shoulders. She was biting her lip and gritting her teeth. She didn't want to have to decide anything.

"Fine. I don't want to go out either. Let's get food and cook dinner. I think we still have a bottle of red on the rack."

Nathalie listed her conditions:

"Will you help me practice my lines while we cook?"

"Yes."

"Will you do all the dishes tomorrow after I go to work?"

"Yes."

"Will you play guitar later?"

"I'll sing to you."

"And you can't sing silly. I want a slow song."

"Done."

"I decide when we go to bed."

"Forget bed. Let's stay up all night and never get tired."

"Stop that."

Back at the apartment, Nathalie dimmed the lights and lit some candles. I put on a King Oliver record, poured us big glasses of wine and toasted Nat cheers.

"Thanks for taking care of the mouse," she said, inviting me to dance. The brassy jazz set the mood perfectly. Boy, we got crazy. Nat started to bounce and twirl around me. Sometimes she'd step away and pretend to tap dance, then she'd lunge forward and make me catch her. She danced everywhere she went, sucked down wine and gave me Harlem kisses—each kiss full of spiced Rioja that trickled warm down my throat as she slid through my arms.

I took the fish fillets we'd purchased out of the fridge. "What costume should I wear?" Nat asked.

"What's the part?"

"The play is very experimental."

"What's it called?" I asked, putting oil on the skillet.

"You'll laugh."

"I won't. Please? I promise," I insisted.

Another glass of wine and she was ready to tell. *"Diary of the Damned,"* she said, naming the play.

I burst out laughing.

"See, I knew you would laugh."

"What bullshit poet wrote that?"

"Stop! It's a good role. I have a monologue."

"I'm sorry," I said, but I couldn't stop laughing.

"Do I have to leave?" Nat sighed, staring me down until I was calm enough for her to tell me about the play. "It's a series of different people's diary entries acted out in short scenes," she explained. "I play Charlotte, a mother who finds out her kid has Muscular Dystrophy."

"Black," I suggested. "Bad news always calls for black."

"You're useless. You know I won't wear black anymore."

"Not even for me?"

"Never."

"Surprise me?"

She slid her copy of the script across the counter and went to her room. I sat down on the stool and skimmed the dialogue while I waited for her to come back. To tell the truth, I liked what I read. The character situations were very melodramatic and con-trived, but scene-wise, I thought the opportunities were rich. The directions for Nathalie's part had her wheeling her poor son around the stage while she plans her day and grieves for her slow-dying child. The whole production, I gathered, hinged on whether or not Nathalie thought Char-lotte's character was strong enough to bear misfortune.

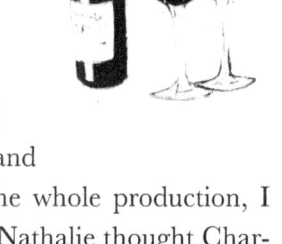

They say the most beautiful women in the world are full of curves. That isn't true. They're full of shadows. Nathalie re-emerged wearing the silkiest silver dress. The V-neck exposed the gentle slope of her chest, the cinnamon circles of her nip-ples and ended in a lacy tie that drew around her waist. Enticing shadows were everywhere, like pockets full of lust.

We kissed and waltzed a little more. I reached inside her dress and cupped her breasts. I kissed her up and down her body. Then I hoisted Nat up on the counter where I found myself between her legs. I dabbled my fingers in her under-wear where it was warm and wet. She said to wait till after dinner, but I wouldn't wait. I had to see her come. I wanted to make her wild.

We finished and washed. By then we were starving. I did most of the cooking while Nat paced back and forth reciting her lines. Whenever a word didn't come out clear, or she read something in monotone I made her repeat her line. Meanwhile, our salmon fillets sizzled and drizzled with lemon and mustard. I chopped lettuce for a salad while the rice boiled and fluffed. Sweet and salty, the room smelled up, and we both laughed at the rumbling noises our stomachs made.

"This looks beautiful," Nathalie said as I garnished everything with ripe dill. I served her, and I don't think we spoke another word until the last gulp of wine was behind us, the food devoured. We spread a blanket on the floor to eat, and when we finished, Nat brought out chocolate and a chilled bottle of port. That was when I told her about the job.

"Five hundred dollars! That's great, Myles." Nat was pleased, but her celebrations were short lived. Her mood changed when she started thinking how we could use the money. "Does this mean you can pay rent this month?" she asked.

Seeing me hesitate, Nat reacted angrily. "Fine. I knew you wouldn't," she huffed.

"But Nat, didn't I already pay you half?"

"That was last month. Remember? And you still owe me for utilities."

"Last month was hard. I thought you cut me a break."

"I'm having a hard time too, Myles. But now you're in the green. Can't you pay your share?" Nat's eyes were piercing. She steamed when I avoided her stare. "What do you want me to say?" she asked. "That it's all fine? Go ahead. Sleep on my bed when I'm not home. Eat my food. Use my dishes. You even finish my shampoo and leave the fucking empty bottles for me to find when I'm in the middle of a shower. Myles, I can't stand this. I'm sorry we slept together. I'm sorry we have fun. But this is my home, and you're basically living here for free. You know I love your writing, and I appreciate you helping me learn my lines, but this isn't fair."

"Nat! Slow down. I never said I wouldn't pay."

"You were suggesting—"

"Come on. You know me. I don't want to pay any more rent than I have to. Who does? I only want to spend my money on fun."

"Fun? You're an ass," she said, flying out of the living room. "Don't come near me. I'm leaving right now."

I chased her around the apartment, trying to take back what I'd said. Finally I trapped her in the bedroom.

"I know that was insensitive. I only wanted to make you laugh," I begged forgiveness. "You've laughed before when I said something like that. Can I have a minute to explain?"

"Fine. One minute. That's it. Then I'm taking a cab to Ben's place."

That was the first time she'd actually said his name. I didn't let it hurt. I knew she was seeing the guy. He was a doctor she'd met through a Jewish dating service. If I could make her laugh, then I knew we'd make up.

"Will you at least sit down?"

"One minute. The clock is ticking."

My first thoughts were all mush, and Nathalie was not impressed. Finally, I mumbled something that stopped her counting down the seconds.

"Earning an extra five hundred bucks a week. That's news. That makes a big difference for us. Can I have one day to enjoy myself before it's all spent? Of course, I'll pay the rent. I only wanted to take you out this weekend. I thought we could wander the city. Maybe even go to the beach. Can't we spend one paycheck on fun? Life's too short."

Nat sniffled, muffling a laugh. I guess there was something funny about the way I'd said all that. Either way she was all emotion now. I could see her lips trembling around the words she wished to speak. Her eyes were red and watering. We were through the worst. She'd have left already if she couldn't forgive me.

"Damn you, Myles, why do you always have to do that?" she cried. "Why do you always make it about life, death, staying up all night and never getting tired? That's too much fun for me. Can't you see? That hurts me. Don't look at me like that. Please don't. You make me feel like I'm no fun."

She was practically choking on tears. Her mascara ran in lines. Finally, her head fell on my chest.

"I'm sorry Nat," I apologized, holding her tight. "But nobody tempts me the same as you. You're my Wicked Witch of the West."

 10:00 P.M., Wednesday, March 5, 2008

Something wasn't right. I let myself back into the building and was halfway upstairs when I noticed that the apartment door was wide open. The TV was blaring.

Was it the Feds? I cocked the Luger and stayed close to the wall as I climbed the rest of the stairs. I couldn't hear any voices, only the TV. I knelt low to the ground and peeked inside through the open door. There had been a struggle. The couch was overturned. Lee's tea mug was shattered. A puddle of brown water lay in front of me, and the potted palm in the corner was toppled.

I moved inside the apartment, ducked behind the couch and pointed the pistol down the hall. When I looked up, Jimmy Stewart stared me in the face on that damned big screen. I found the remote and lowered the volume. Someone in the other room was struggling to breathe.

"You coward," uttered a deranged voice.

I tiptoed toward the guest room. Keeping the Luger below my chin, I stole a look inside. Ethan had his back to me. He towered over Lee, choking the kid's neck. With his other hand, he held a pistol to Lee's head.

"Damn you, Lee," Ethan shouted, his hands shaking as he rolled the cold gun over Lee's chubby cheeks and floppy lips. "Why'd you leave your post? How can you be so selfish? Now we're all fucked. That was the deal. Murphy will kill us."

Lee said nothing. His eyes were glazed with fear.

"I should kill you," Ethan grew redundant. "We made a pact."

I crept closer. I was a foot away from Ethan when I put the Luger to his ear.

"Let him go, Ethan. Drop the gun or I'll shoot."

"What the fuck?"

"Drop the gun."

Ethan didn't realize how hard he was squeezing Lee's neck. The kid was gasping for air and foaming at the mouth.

"Ethan, let go. You're choking him."

"He left his post, Myles. Nobody could leave. He's a traitor."

"Ethan, you fire that gun, and I'll shoot."

Ethan started to laugh.

"I'm dead anyway."

"Stop. Professor Murphy was bluffing about the pact."

"No, he wasn't. He'll kill me sooner or later. He'll kill you, too."

"Enough! Put the gun down. Lee can't breathe."

"No. I can't. Lee left. We made a pact. One of us has to kill."

"Yes, Ethan, but look where you are. You left too."

Typical New York
(August 2007)

The first week I was in Professor Murphy's employ, nearly everyone I made plans to interview blew me off. First there was the awkward call with Ethan. "Myles? I've thought about this a lot," he said. "We're not friends. We've never been friends. I don't see why I should have to talk to you. I know I'm supposed to—for the movement—but I refuse."

Ethan was right. We'd never gotten along in high school. I couldn't blame him for not wanting to be interviewed. Next, Landon stood me up twice before I realized the meeting was never going to happen. I stopped by Sam's office in Midtown one afternoon at a time he'd scheduled, but he, too, had to cut the meeting short when an important client called.

Frustrated, I turned to Ari and Lee. The two met me at a downtown bar close to Lee's work at Ground Zero. They were excited to play Ari's game, "Big Echo," but that was a strange way to talk to someone. Each player was tasked with choosing a prompt and improvising a monologue about their subject, all under a two-minute time limit. Categories could be dramatic or comical.

"Grandparents?" I said, reading the prompt written on the crumpled piece of paper I'd drawn from Ari's hat.

"Don't hold back," Ari encouraged. "Say anything that comes to mind."

I talked about how my grandfather, who lived outside the city, was sick with cancer and immediately apologized when my two minutes were up. I thought my speech was boring and redundant, but Ari and Lee were obsessively supportive, sounding phony as hell.

"You did great, Myles," Ari said. "I liked the part about your grandfather's war record."

"I think you repeated yourself only once. That was very good for your first try," Lee reassured. I laughed and told them I didn't need therapy, but that I thought the game was fun.

True story. More often than not, Big Echo *was* amusing. When Lee chose the category "Sex in your childhood bed," he became incredibly sarcastic. "First of all, it's the shit," he announced. Afterward, it was like watching stand-up comedy.

The game turned serious, however, when Ari chose the topic, "oil." Then a hush of intrigue swept over the three of us. The category was rich and complicated. Every tangent peered into Ari's tormented vision of the world. He indicted politicians and entrepreneurs. He spoke about the people he had met in the backcountry out west; how their pain at the pump had no bounds. According to Ari, the country was ignorant of the hole the government had dug for itself in Iraq, and the President's lopsided and desperate deals with the Saudis only made the situation worse. "We'll never be free again," he closed his tirade. "Our generation was sold to slavery."

"Why are you in this group?" I asked Lee when Ari went to get us another round, "You weren't in the wars."

"I almost joined. I sympathize with veterans," he said, a hint of anger in his voice.

"Then why this group? There are other anti-war organizations you could join."

"We're the only group that's actively fighting back against the war," Lee answered.

I asked what, exactly, they planned to do, but he hushed up quick. Then he lapsed into another monologue, reciting those famous lines from British passports; "Her Britannic Majesty's Secretary of State Requests and requires in the Name of Her Majesty..." Ari returned with the beers and joined in.

When they'd finished, Lee explained the reference. "Murphy learned that spying for the IRA. He made us memorize the lines. Just goes to show you how the world is caught up following propaganda slogans. Somehow, that term, 'her Britannic Majesty,' is as weighted as the sound of the fat lady singing the Star Spangled Banner before a ball game. Beautiful propaganda stirs hearts. She makes you want to serve."

I could tell they were quoting their professor.

"Words like that are compelling," Ari filled in the rest. "You fall in line and do what's expected, but now nobody can afford principles or patriotism anymore. Not after this war. We can't trust our allegiances. The lies are piled too high. That's why we've got to use more force and expose their rhetoric."

"And then what?"

"We'll blow it up," Ari said with a strange smirk on his face. "We're going to unravel the conspiracies surrounding 9/11, show how the country was duped into war. Murphy is going to bring the government crashing down and Bush begging for forgiveness."

"Why does Murphy want that? He didn't fight in Iraq."

"Advocating for an honorable end to the wars and proper recognition for veterans is a just cause, whether or not you saw active duty," Ari repeated Murphy's sympathies.

Lee, however, was more aggressive. "Murphy has our best interests at heart," he insisted, ignoring my question. "Why don't you give him the benefit of the doubt?"

Chris, at least, was a little more forthcoming. He lived nearby on the West side. One morning, before he went to work, we met for coffee. The war, he explained, had confirmed his ambition to become an artist and an activist. His mediums of choice were charcoal and pastels, and he went to great lengths to explain his style in relation to the group's meeting place on 75th Street.

"What we're trying to do is stage a scene. We've got to make that apartment, that street, the whole East Side, a mirror for the country to look into. Remember the music? I've told you how today's music doesn't suit us. We've got to give the country something else to look at and listen to. Something that tells the truth, finally."

Chris' lecture was disjointed, but I found his art interesting.

"You see this one?" he asked about a charcoal sketch in the notebook he'd brought along. "I call it *American Blood.*" The picture showed a slightly open door to a raided home, stuck in a Baghdad alley. A wounded soldier's blood spilled out of the entrance, and a sly cat—striped like Duke Ellington—lapped the puddle up as though it were a saucer of milk.

"The blood spills are the only evidence of the government's deceit. Nobody forgets scenes like that. The trouble is, the criminals in Washington and in the Pentagon don't want us to see anything that reminds us of the wars. They want us to go shopping, for fuck's sake. Talk to Landon or Ethan about Dorzene," Chris said, suggesting I inquire about the powerful post-traumatic stress drugs being prescribed to veterans. "If you don't have the strength of mind to get clean when you first get back, then the government is more than happy to numb you up. You'll never talk about what happened over there again."

"How are the veterans treated?" I asked, finishing my coffee.

Chris hastily explained the ninety-day return from service program that the army had implemented to help soldiers re-adapt to civilian life. He laughed at their rituals and procedures.

"The program is purely for show. You have a meeting every thirty days with an Army psychiatrist. Then you receive a phony 'freedom party' to celebrate your civilian status. What a joke. Seriously, I don't know how they expect that to get a man to open up about the horrors of war, and you're certainly not cured of PTS when it's over."

"Is that why Ethan won't talk to me?"

Chris shrugged his shoulders and looked at his watch. He had to catch a train, so I walked him to the subway.

"Look, it's simple. The government wants to forget about us," he explained before going down the steps to the underground. "Pardon my pun, they want the Afghan swept clean, and they're obsessed with the illusion that they can get away with murder. I don't know if everyone will talk to you. I don't even know if we all agree on everything concerning the war. So don't get caught up on guys like Ethan who are emotional meatheads."

"What *do* you want? What are your demands?"

Chris smiled. "Vindication," he answered.

"But you all volunteered. How can you demand that?"

"We want our sacrifice taken seriously," Chris said, launching into a speech. "You don't know how empty life is for us now that we're back home. People take us for granted. The American people never had to see or feel the wars if they didn't want to, and that means they can't understand what we went through. That's why Murphy's and our work

 is essential. We have to make noise now. Do something that hits home. Otherwise, Americans will never know the truth. The wars are unpopular. Mistakes were made. We understand the public's anger, but it's not our fault."

Chris forgot to breathe. His face was turning red. Still, he continued speaking out. "The men I served with are heroes," he stressed. Nobody would be free if it weren't for our sacrifice. People forget we were attacked on 9/11. We had to defend ourselves. Now it's time to end the wars responsibly and with honor. Write that down and you'll get the guys talking," Chris promised.

I walked away annoyed. Why couldn't anyone talk specifics? Why was Murphy their leader? Without a chronological and consistent war story, I didn't know how to frame their mission. By the time I met Dylan later that week, I was doubtful that I'd earned my salary.

We sat on a bench in Battery Park, eating lunch. As we watched the ferry circle the Statue of Liberty, Dylan brushed crumbs off his suit and tried to reassure me.

"Come on. You've made a good start. Give yourself some credit."

"No. I've done shit work this week. I don't even feel right taking the money now."

Dylan started laughing. He didn't believe for a second that I wouldn't take my pay.

"I'm serious," I said. "I feel useless."

"Don't worry," Dylan reassured. "Murphy is good for the money."

"What's that supposed to mean?"

"Myles, treat this like any desk job. Some weeks you're productive, others you're negligent."

"Come on. Murphy will see through that. The way Lee describes him, he's a regular double agent."

"Relax. You're over-analyzing. We're all on Murphy's payroll for bullshit jobs. Take Ethan, for example. What does he do for us besides picket in Times Square now and then?"

"And Murphy pays him?"

"The same rate as the rest of us."

"Where does he get the money?"

"Beats me. Maybe I don't want to know," Dylan answered, laughing sheepishly. He stopped when he saw my face. Growing defensive, "Where's your sense of opportunism?" he asked. "Believe me, this is a good deal. I know it's a little freaky at first. You feel bought. But once that money starts flowing everything changes. Finally you can afford to live in this city."

Dylan had few regrets. He didn't care whether the money was honest. All that mattered was that he had work and that Murphy's exclusive club of investors continued fast tracking his career in banking.

I shook my head. I was tempted to ask Dylan for a spontaneous, Big Echo monologue on corporate bonuses, but I didn't want to hear him brag about the money he was making. Instead, I decided to go uptown after lunch and talk to the boss.

Professor Murphy's chuckles were sharper than Dylan's, but in their own way cheerful.

"I thought they might resist a tad. But they'll be telling you," Murphy said, standing up. He examined some titles on his shelves, then returned to his seat. Rummaging in his desk drawer, Murphy produced several, crisp, hundred-dollar bills and put them in an envelope.

"You'll excuse me, Myles," he said. "I've another meeting waiting. You'll get to it, won't you? Here's six hundred."

Stunned, I took the money.

"There's a slight advance for you," Murphy explained as I counted the bills in disbelief. "Most the boys need a little starting push. You might try announcing yourself uninvited or following one of the lads home after work. Why not put a little journalistic pressure on? The boys, they'll come around. You'll see. Keep playing Ari's game if it helps them talk. You never know what echoes in a man's soul."

Murphy patted my shoulder and showed me out of his office. Down the hall, Ari and Landon were sitting on the sofa. Ari was surprised to see me. He sprung to his feet and wouldn't look me in the face. His companion, meanwhile, didn't twitch a muscle.

"What are you doing here?" Ari asked. I said I needed some information about a few of the members. My answer didn't satisfy him. He looked nervous, and he kept eying the leather briefcase that was lying on the table.

"Can we take a walk?" I asked.

"I can't talk now. We're running late," Ari said.

"Will you be long?"

"I don't know."

"Let's get a drink later. What do you say?"

"I can't. We have some business to take care of."

"I'll wait," I suggested, following Ari back down the hall.

"You need to leave," Ari said, slipping inside Murphy's office and locking me out.

"I'll be in the park," I told the closed door. "There's some writing I want to do."

Rejected, I wandered back down the hall.

"What about you? How about a drink?" I asked Landon.

I wondered if his hearing was damaged in a blast. He didn't react. The hulking man continued tracing the lines of his scars. Then he reached down beside the sofa and brought a pair of soundproof stereo headphones out of his bag. He plugged the jack into his smart phone and began scrolling through music. I took that as my cue to leave.

Six hundred dollars. Joel would be jealous. Not even a dealer turns so much profit from so little effort. I could forget Ari and Landon's bizarre behavior easily enough. That money was burning a hole in my pocket. I thought I'd buy Nathalie a present. Maybe a hat? Nat loved accessories. With the extra money, I could get one for myself too. After all, Nathalie was always telling me I needed props to make my work go. Her theory was, "you're never in character until you're in costume." Before auditions, she'd pretend that every day was dress up day. What the hell, I felt inspired and I thought I'd give Nat's trick a try.

On my way to the park, I kicked the book around a bit in my thoughts. I knew I'd overwritten the first chapters. I'd invented all the periphery characters, but I was afraid to introduce Ari as himself and also his younger brother, Jeremy, as the wild card catalyst for all the novel's action. The setting, on the other hand, was well established. I had imagined a bar back home in Ithaca and a couple of regular characters who were all acting lost in the aftermath of 9/11. The idea was to have somebody show up, somebody dramatic—just like Jeremy. He'd pull them all out of their idle slump.

The trouble was, whenever I set out to write about Ari, he never seemed himself. I remembered him passive and more accommodating than he had become. I couldn't reconcile Ari's new, assertive, even aggressive personality with the character I knew on paper. As I imagined the next few scenes, Jeremy stole the show. The kid would start a bluegrass band and convince all the main characters to follow him on a cross-country tour.

I was impatient to start writing, but I wanted to run the idea by Ari first. When I tried calling him, he didn't pick up. I decided to quit wandering and choose a destination. The hat store I liked was in the upper thirties. Excited, I clenched that wad of cash and hurried down Broadway, through Midtown.

News, news, news! Fast facts streaked along their ticker-tracks, announcing the gathering crisis. Spiking oil prices, the housing bubble, fraudulent banking, even pirates! Then the breaking intensity of the headlines petered out, and the news ran soft—baseball trades, celebrity scandals, advertisements, a blank space, back to the top. Spelled together, the dominating fear of the day was *Recession!* That word alone symbolized a brewing, perfect storm whose vanguard clouds passed daily over Manhattan. Worse than the war, the horrible idea of losing confidence in money swirled in the distance like an unpredictable tornado. Clueless analysts, meanwhile, hyped the fear. They spun their wheels in muck, offering worthless advice—which market, which bank, what homes, the tempest would strike first.

I'd seen their target before but never given it much thought. Of course, I didn't know yet that Professor Murphy would designate the little Army Recruitment Center in the middle of Times Square for demolition. At first glance, it hardly seemed like the malevolent symbol his followers made it out to be. Later, however, when I was more familiar with the hated army slogans and propaganda that Murphy and his men tirelessly condemned, I began to understand why they chose Times Square to make their stand.

Dwarfed by the Midtown skyscrapers, the small office was wrapped in recruitment posters promoting the nation's soldiers as the world's sole defenders of freedom. "I want you!" they stated on behalf of Uncle Sam. "Be all that you can be!" Didn't the culture of the square demand those fighting slogans? The corporate and tourist atmosphere was conquering. Look up, look down, look all around; the crowd cheers for capitalism! One point six million people wandering through the jam each day. They kneel to that big Panasonic television and the crystal ball crown on top. They kneel to the Nasdaq, the Dow, the pulse and power of seemingly unlimited credit.

"Our great escape," Ari had described the place during his monologue on oil. "Salute the flag," he'd said, "and in the meanwhile, thank God for your distractions."

He was right. Now I saw how eyes bulge at the apparition of two M&M's smiling and waving. All that gaudy advertising. My heart felt yanked in contradictory directions. Bad news could spin in circles, predict capitalism in its death throes and sound every alarm, but in Times Square I couldn't give a damn. True poetry and perfect irony, New York was a great tragedy suspended on big-boom-bubbles about to burst. No city in the world has ever made me want to laugh and cry so much.

"Myles? Is that you?" someone called from behind a crowd of tourists. I couldn't believe my luck. It was Ethan.

"What the hell are you doing here?" I asked him.

"Protesting."

We shook hands, and he handed me one of his flyers. Then he searched his pockets for a cigarette. He grew jittery when his hand came up empty.

"You see that part about dishonorable discharge?" he asked, pointing in the flyer to the testimony of a soldier who was court-martialed because he refused to serve in Iraq. "How can you do that to a soldier? Lieutenant Ehren Watada thought he'd volunteered for a just cause. Then the govern-

ment changed war aims. We thought we were going to be liberators. We thought we were defending Americans. The war
has nothing to do with any of that anymore. It's a pointless
crusade against Islam and an oil grab. Want to know what
I think? I wouldn't be surprised if 9/11 was an inside job,"
Ethan said. I didn't question his conclusion. That emboldened
him. Now he gestured at the recruitment office as though the
men inside were personally responsible for his deception.

"Look at that kid going in there now. He has no idea,"
Ethan said, pointing to the young black man who was waiting
at the door for an interview.

Suddenly, Ethan pushed me aside. "You're going to trust an
organization that lies to you?" he heckled the recruit. "Bet you
think you're going to be a hero! Shooting Arabs over there. I bet
you think that will be fun. Wake up! You dumb fuck."

Maybe if Ethan wore his uniform, he'd be more persuasive.
He looked like a redneck in his sweat-stained wife beater. The
recruit merely regarded him another New York crazy, shouting
out the ramblings of his unhinged mind. The kid slipped inside
the office, but Ethan didn't stop his rant.

"This country doesn't give a damn about you," he shouted, louder than before. "You'll die over there!"

Ethan would have continued railing against the "industrial military complex" until his voice ran out, but several police-
men were approaching.

"Come on Ethan," I warned him. "Let's take a break."
He spit on the sidewalk and seemed to shrink back inside himself. The cops came closer.

"Got a cigarette, Myles?" he asked me. I rummaged in my
pocket, but before I could pull one out, Ethan changed his mind.

"Forget it," he said. "Let's get out of here. What I really want
is some Chinese food. I'm hungry as hell, and I can't watch this."

 10:15 P.M., Wednesday, March 5, 2008

Lee fled the apartment the second Ethan let go of his neck. The door slammed. Now I wanted Ethan's gun.

"Go on," Ethan said, staring at my weapon. "Shoot me, Myles. It's your responsibility." I thought he was about to collapse.

"You're mad," I said. "I won't shoot you. Put the gun on the table. Let's talk."

"Myles, you'll have to do it for him."

"Who are you talking about?"

"Murphy. I can't stand the paranoia. Please, Myles, shoot. I trust you. Kill me now and I won't suffer waiting."

"Stop talking that way."

"Go on. You can do it. You're a writer, aren't you? Make it poetic. Aim right here," Ethan said, pointing to his heart. That was the most composed I'd ever heard him. There was only one thing I could do. Slowly, I lowered my gun. We each took a breath.

"Ethan, You know I won't shoot you. If Murphy comes after you, we'll get him first."

"The hell we will," Ethan shouted, seizing the moment to point his gun at me. I was back against the wall. That was dumb. I should never have given up my advantage. Now everything was on Ethan's terms.

"You have no idea what Murphy is, do you?" Ethan roared. "He's a terrorist!"

The bully was in my face. He snatched the Luger out of my hand and tossed it on the floor. "Who says he won't come after you first?" he snarled.

I couldn't speak.

"Are you serious? You never even considered that possibility, did you? Don't you know what Murphy did to those Colombians up in Harlem? The ones who made the bombs."

Scenes flashed through my mind. I remembered the briefcase Ari couldn't take his eyes off that day I intruded on his meeting with Murphy. He, the professor and their strongman Landon had all gone uptown together after I left. Was the briefcase full of money?

Ethan pressed his gun into my temple. The pain made me dizzy.

"How could you not know?"

"Murphy didn't tell me everything, Ethan. He doesn't trust me. That's why he didn't send me downtown with you guys tonight."

"Jesus Christ, you played the fool. Murphy murdered everyone in that cartel. He's an IRA terrorist, Myles, the real thing. They call him 'The Wolf.' He spent ten years in a British Prison. There's no mercy when Murphy kills. Everybody dies badly. He poisoned two guys, stabbed another. Want to know how he did in their ring-leader? Jesus, you still don't believe me, do you? That even made the news. *Drug Lord Burned Alive in Jersey Car Explosion. Police Suspect Sabotage.* I remember the headlines. You're wondering how I know Murphy killed them? I'll tell you. The sick bastard left a charred thumb on my nightstand last night."

I didn't say anything. How could I? Ethan kept up his rant.

"Now do you understand why I'm scared? We're traitors and Murphy is better trained than we are. We don't stand a chance. Unless we take our own lives, his vengeance will be torture. You trust me, Myles, don't you? I'll shoot you clean."

The gun was pointed to my chest. Ethan was very close. His breath stank and his eyes were bloodshot. I was trembling.

"What You Do to Love?"
(August 2007)

Ethan took me to his favorite restaurant in Chinatown, a dump off Canal Street. The basement restaurant stank of burned oil, the tables were slick with grease, and the air was damp.

"How did you ever find this place?" I asked. Ethan grinned, pointing toward our waitress. Lu, his "little chink," as he called her, was making rounds with the teakettle. She was like a dumpling—yellow skin, small breasts and a plump bottom.

"You ever get the fever?" he asked, admitting a fetish.

I didn't answer.

"My god," he said. "Look at her bend. Underneath that skirt, she's got one tight, hairy twat. Makes me wish I'd been in Nam. Man, I'd have fun over there. I wouldn't be with Josie. I'll tell you that. All those exotic companion whores. The girls in Iraq were a waste of time. Sure they had those big, exotic, Persian eyes, but everything else was covered. What's under the burka stays under the burka. You don't want anybody going jihad on your ass for messing around with a Muslim woman. But I'd love to have a girl like

Lu. Just look at those teeth, Myles. Nice little daggers, aren't they?" Ethan rambled, using his fingers to demonstrate the sensation of little bites and pinches the whole way up and down the shaft of his cock. "Bet you'd love to have her mouth your junk."

The girl was coming our way. I nodded to warn him.

"Etan? Love. Who yo friend?" Lu asked, drawing a notepad out of her apron to take our order. "Okay, My-o you like Chin-ee food? What yo favorite dish?"

Lu's temperament was sweet and sour. I laughed, watching Ethan drool over her. In the end, however, I knew his lust for her was harmless.

"One or two order? Ok, spicy pwan, wonton soup, egg woll, beef wit brocc-li and cwunchy chicken-cash-oo."

The place was BYOB. As soon as Lu went into the kitchen, we unscrewed the tops on the two bottles of cheap, Old Viejo white wine we'd bought at the bodega next door.

"One for me, one for you," Ethan said with that same dirty grin on his face. We clinked bottles and poured ourselves glasses.

"How was the food over there?" I managed to get in a pertinent question as we broke apart our wooden chopsticks.

Ethan grinned. "Best I ever ate," he said. "The taxpayer is a damn good cook."

"You mean Halliburton?" I asked, aware of the immense contracts the corporation had received from the government.

"Man, we were royalty over there. Spoiled rotten. We had Maine lobsters delivered to the base. We had steaks, fillet mignon, scallops, anything we asked for. If we'd been in New York, I'd have racked up a hundred dollar bill each night, easy. Everything was served buffet style, and it was all for free. We must be the only army in the history of the world ever fed like that."

Lu brought out our first tray of food, and we dug in.

"You ever hear of DMT?" Ethan asked, chewing loudly as he refilled my glass with the too-sweet wine. I shook my head.

"That's the fatal enzyme," he explained. "You know, the hormone the body excretes in the seconds before death. Taken as a hallucinogen, you see lots of colorful squiggles. Anyway, Jim got me some. When we came down from the high, he took me out for a fancy meal. I'm telling you, the stuff was magic. Finally I could taste again."

"You can't taste your food?"

"Not anymore. Not since I've been back in the States."

"Have you seen a doctor?"

"What for? I'm healthy. I think that's one of the symptoms of being back. You get numb. When I ate every meal with fear in my gut, thinking it might be my last, I tasted more. That's all. Somehow I felt more alive over there."

Ethan was nostalgic for a particular meal he'd had the night before they took Baghdad. As he smiled and waved his arms above the table, gesticulating about the luxurious dining in the service, I couldn't help noticing the thick pink scar that crossed the bulging blue veins on his wrist. When Ethan saw me staring, he kicked me hard under the table.

"What was that for?"

"Don't look at me that way. These scars? They're not what you think. Besides, who the fuck are you? Why should I tell you anything about what happened to me over there?"

"I think you're dying to tell me." I shot back.

Ethan was furious. His eyes refused to blink, and his buzzed, blonde hair stood on edge.

"I think you want to tell because we all remember what a kid you were before the war," I kept pushing. "You're embarrassed. You were that guy who played so many violent video games you had to go to Iraq, just to find out what it feels like to kill someone. Am I right?"

"No. You've got me all wrong, Myles. You're way off base."

"Fine. Prove me wrong. Now's your chance. That's what I think of you. I'm sorry, but I'm being honest. We *all* thought you were a joke the way you acted when you enlisted. Promising us dead Iraqis at a party? Nobody wanted anything to do with you and your war. Tell me what really happened and change my mind. I'll write everything down for Murphy. Then everyone will know your story."

"Fuck you for judging me. I don't give a damn about Murphy's magazine, and I know you're a hack reporter."

I started to get up, but Ethan grabbed my arm and forced me back into my seat.

"Don't go," he begged, some new fear sweeping over him.

"Don't kick me," I said, freeing my arm. Ethan put his hands up in surrender.

"Just promise me you won't make shit up," he asked.

Soon we were trading, one bite of dumpling for one tidbit of the story, one slurp of soup for another part of the picture. I'd heard war stories before, but never one so detailed. The soldiers I met in Israel had seen horrible things in their country's wars, but they narrated their stories differently. Accounts of Gaza and Lebanon were related with a certain shrug of the shoulders and a cool hit from a joint. Israelis feel the inevitability and necessity of their service more than Americans do. Growing up amid constant tensions that can lead to war, they know what to expect from their enemies and become hardened in advance. Ethan, on the other hand, was tragically scarred. Everything he encountered in Iraq, it seemed, surprised him. The war had chewed up his innocence and confused his character. There was no chronology to what he related. He bounced back and forth between events and blurred memories.

"I was in a transport," he remembered. "We were in the desert. Fighters were streaking across the sky from Kuwait. Shock and awe, baby. We were testing everything in our arsenal, precision missiles and stealth bombers. Suddenly you'd hear a roar. Then the ground would quake. There was a covering over the armored truck. I couldn't see much besides the dusty road. It was hot and dry. I was stinking in my uniform and boots. Our helmets knocked together as we rolled over the sand dunes. Some guys were nervous. They kept checking their weapons and ammo. I knew there wasn't going to be much of a fight. We were the Iraqis' liberators. That's what everyone believed, but I remember the last news reports before we invaded. A shopkeeper was holding a pistol. 'It's not to fight the Americans,' he said. 'It's for when they leave.' Anyway, there we were, driving into hell. That's when my commander announced *Operation Crown Jewel*. 'Secure the Rumailah oil fields!' orders came in over the radio. Jesus Christ, the war was all about oil. Once we'd invaded, they didn't try to hide their aims."

"Next, they've got us driving through the streets of Baghdad with trucks full of food and medicine. I go to hand out an MRE. That's a Meal Ready to Eat. There's a woman in a burka. She's holding her son's hand and running behind the truck. I'm leaning out the back of the truck, trying to reach out to them, but we're driving too fast, and I'm afraid to throw the package. Suddenly my commanding officer pulls me back. 'Are you crazy?" he says. "They could have IED's. "Besides, this is not a humanitarian mission.' The war only got more confusing. Especially when the insurgents started sniping. My friend Pat got shot in the forehead when we were operating a checkpoint. Suddenly, his blood was all over my face. Things like that happened all the time. The insurgents were hiding out in Fallujah. We had to take the city, and the fighting was fierce. My friend's unit got ambushed when the battle started. They hid out in a school until relief arrived. We were going door to door. Some buildings were booby-trapped. I saw guys get blown off their feet. We threw cans of tear gas, but that didn't stop the insurgents. They kept on coming. Our boys had to fire and it wasn't always clear where the enemy was. A lot of civilians got caught in the crossfire. Afterward, nobody talked about what happened. My friend doesn't even remember hearing his gun go off. Jesus, the fighting went on and on for months."

"Are you going to finish that?" Ethan interrupted his speech, pointing at my bottle of wine. His was empty. Mine was near full. I pushed the juice toward him.

"But you want to know about my scar, don't you?" he asked, taking a big gulp.

"It's a point of interest."

"Hey, do me a favor? Don't believe everything people say about me, Myles. I didn't try to commit suicide."

"Nobody told me that," I lied.

"This was an honest accident. A grenade went off. I dove for cover. My sleeve got caught on a piece of sheet metal. When I pulled it loose, I cut my wrist. That's what happened. The Army sent a medical officer to evaluate me. I was shell-shocked. As soon as I'd healed, they wanted to put me right back in the field."

"And you didn't mind going back?"

Ethan didn't know what to say. The restaurant had emptied. There was nothing left to drink, and Lu had gone into the kitchen. His story was a lead weight.

He grasped his forehead, hiding his eyes behind his big hands. "I've never told anybody this. Not even Josie." He mumbled, waiting for me to nod.

"When I was in the hospital, I remembered scenes. Or I hallucinated. I don't know. I had no idea what was happening."

"Were you on pain relievers?"

"Valium mostly and something for PTS. Dorzene, I think."

"What did you see?"

Ethan shook his head and started picking at a callus on his palm. "I don't know if any of this really happened. Do you understand?" he asked. "You can write whatever you want, but that doesn't mean it's true. Smells trigger flashbacks. I'd been lying in bed for days. I smelled some chemical, something acidic that burned my nostrils. When I was drowsy, I'd nod off. That's when I'd see the man's face. His nose was crushed from a fall, and his eye was gouged out from a bullet. Dark red blood was clotted in his white beard. I think I was the one who shot him. He stank. I remember that. He'd been dead for over a day. Flies were buzzing, and I was cut off from my platoon. We were buried in rubble. I'd thought he was a sniper. Dressed like that, how could I have known he was a civilian? The fighting was street to street. When Pat got hit, his blood splattered all over me. I couldn't see. I started shooting everywhere. I ended up pinned down by enemy fire and face to face with that dead Iraqi, rotting in the sun. I'll never forget that smell. I didn't know what to do. Then the ground started shaking as the helicopters approached and more grenades went off. There was a blast. I saw squiggling lights, then blacked out from the pain. I found out later that it was friendly fire. Fucking friendly fire! Now everybody is wondering about these scars on my wrist, and whether I tried to kill myself? Myles, to tell you the truth, I don't have a clue how that scar got there. All I know is that when I woke up in a hospital bed, I wanted to go home, but the fucking army wouldn't let me."

Ethan was pounding his fist on the table. Lu rushed over to our table and sat beside him.

"What you do to Love?" she asked me in her broken tongue, blaming me with her eyes. "Why Et-an cry? What you do to Love?"

 10:30 P.M., Wednesday, March 5, 2008

There was noise. Ethan pressed his gun deep into my temple. I saw squiggling lights.

"Shh," he snarled, making me duck behind the piano. We held our breath. Sam and Jim barged into the common room as though they were the Dukes stumbling aboard Huck's raft.

"Jesus, look at this mess," one told the other.

"Murphy's already been here. Damn, we should have hid the money somewhere else."

"Where the hell is Myles?"

They called out my name a dozen times, but they were too lazy to search all the apartment's nooks and crannies.

"He's not here," Sam reassured Jim.

"Good. Murphy must have nabbed the rat. Hurry. Find the briefcase and let's split."

They began rummaging in a closet.

"If Murphy found the briefcase, we're finished. I told you we shouldn't have hidden the passports with the money. Now how will we get out?" I heard Jim say.

"Shut up. It's here. I hid the money right under their noses."

"This is taking too long," Jim complained when files spilled on the floor. "I won't rest till I've got my money and am safe in Canada. Then I never want to see you again. Did you hear me? I swear to God. I don't know why I ever trusted you. You're a total fuck up."

Sam let him finish before he pulled out the briefcase. Immediately Jim perked up.

"You've found it? Thank God! Quick, open it."

We heard the couches scrape against the floor as they righted the overturned furniture and spread their business out on the coffee table. Then we listened to them count the money. Each thousand-dollar increment they mentioned made Ethan's eyebrows twitch, the numbers ringing in his head like a cash register.

"What do you want to do?" I whispered.

Ethan shushed me, pressing his gun back into my temple. Sam and Jim were arguing.

"That's all? You said five million. Where's the other million I asked for in Euros?"

"I couldn't get the Euros. So we're a little short. No big deal. Four million is plenty. Besides, what are you worried about? I'm the one with a wife and kid to smuggle out."

"You're skimming me, aren't you? I should have known."

"I'm not skimming. Look, there are two even piles. You're getting out of here with a fortune."

"You said five. I want my five."

"Jimmy, you're being a baby. Let this go. You know it's more than enough money. You can have tea in London tomorrow, and a beer in Paris that same afternoon. Have a little humility will you? Four million is more than enough. They're going to lynch somebody soon for what's going on with the banks and

Wall Street. Come on, we both know what's coming. That's a lot of borrowed money right there."

Jim couldn't get over the loss so easily. The market's recent ups and downs had rattled his confidence. He'd become accustomed to losing money, but each vanished sum still hurt his ego. "I can't believe you're shorting me, Sam," he said, breathing heavily. Then he began to pace, shouting, "It's my money, for God's sake. Without me, you'd have nothing. Remember that. We used my hedge fund and my investment strategy. I made you all rich boys, didn't I? I took Murphy's cash, and I quadrupled it. I did all the hard work. All you did was hold the regulators off with your legal tricks. I could have done everything myself. To hell with you. I don't owe you anything!"

Then Jim pulled his gun.

"Jimmy, put that down. You don't mean it," Sam said, falling over himself in shock. He never imagined short, balding, Jim Cohen, would pull a gun. "Jim? Fifty-fifty. That's what we agreed. I should have told you earlier about the Euros. I had some people to pay off. I thought there would be more to split, but then the market took a dip, and I ran out of time. I was going to tell you, honest."

"But you didn't tell me. You left this to the last minute. How do I know you didn't skim the top? Why should I trust you?"

Ethan didn't let Sam think for a second. He leapt from our hiding place as though he'd received desperate, fight to the finish orders and charged into the other room. When he lunged, he scratched my neck with his pistol. I touched the gash. There was blood. No time to clot the wound. I grabbed the Luger and followed Ethan. There was a crash as he knocked the gun out of Jim's hand. Next, Ethan head-butted Sam and pinned them both to the floor. Soon he was standing over the two bleeding cowards, waving his gun. Green bills were raining down.

Last Call
(August 2007)

Ethan was drunk. When we left the restaurant, he could hardly stand up straight, but he had his mind set on finding a Chinese whore to screw.

"Jim will pay," he insisted. "He'll pay for yours too."

Outside, I suggested he get a cab home and sleep it off.

"Fuck off," Ethan growled, pushing me around and calling me a mother. Not my problem. I gave him my cigarettes and wished him luck on his bender. Then I called Ari. We made plans to meet at a bar near my place.

"Ethan showed you his midnight crawl, I take it?" Ari said, amused to learn of our encounter. "Poor Josie. She doesn't know he has the fever for Asians."

The Upper West Side bar was full of Columbia students. Ari swiveled on his stool, laughing.

"You've been everywhere today, haven't you? Uptown. Downtown. Don't you work? What about the novel?"

"I used to have a rule. Never write when I'm angry. Now, whenever I have time to write, I'm always upset," I said, still trying to accept parts of Ethan's story.

"So the book is angry?" Ari asked.

"Not exactly. Actually I want it to come across optimistic

and patriotic. But that feels forced. I mean it's all bad news these days. The war, the economy. There's been ten years of bad news already. How can anyone write a hopeful novel?"

"I guess that's the beauty of a book. The project provides escape. But since when did you give yourself so many rules?"

I didn't answer. Instead, I looked for an excuse. "The musical element frustrates me. I can't write this book without knowing how the band sounds."

Ari swished beer around in his mouth, thinking.

"Maybe you only need to suggest sounds and let the reader decide what they hear," he said, waiting for me to nod approval before he continued. "Are you still basing a character on my brother? Yes? You should know that Jeremy is unpredictable when he plays. He has his own style, and he improvises a lot. I don't think I could describe his sound if I wanted to. How about I get you one of his CD's. Would that help?"

"Perhaps," I said. Then I changed the subject entirely. "Are you going to explain where you've been all night? You were awfully secretive earlier. What the hell did you have to do up in Harlem? It's 1:00 AM."

"Murphy will let you know when he feels we can trust you."

That stabbed, yet I was more curious than hurt. I thought a couple more drinks would pry the story out of him, but I was wrong. Ari was steadfast.

"Cut it out, Myles," he said. "I can't tell you."

When I pressed him again he threatened to leave. After that, we hardly spoke. Our moods clashed until Ari apologized.

"I'm sorry, but you understand, don't you? At the end of the day, I'm sure Murphy will tell you everything you want to know. First you have to build trust."

I put my hand up for him to stop. I understood perfectly. Ari didn't trust me.

"Thank you," he said, relaxing. "By the way, I appreciate your coming back uptown to meet me. It's been a hell of a day." He rubbed his red eyes under his glasses and rested his head in his hands. "My brother isn't coming," he murmured.

"I thought that was all worked out?"

"Jeremy canceled."

"Where was he?"

"Ireland. He went there after he dropped out last year."

"Jeremy didn't finish school? You never told me that."

Ari shrugged his shoulders. "My parents were furious," he said. "But Jer's doing all right now."

"This was supposed to be the first time he'd visited?"

Ari nodded. "We were going to surprise the rest of the family, but he canceled the ticket I bought him this morning. It's a shame. I was looking forward to seeing him. We had concert tickets at the Bowery."

"Jesus, Ar. How much are you out?"

"Seven hundred. Look, I'm over it. I had money. Jeremy didn't. It's important to me that he knows he has a way to get home if he ever needs. The Euro is almost one to two now, and you know my brother, Jer's always hurting for cash. I guess he felt bad taking my money. Or, maybe he just needs more time over there. He's playing a lot of music."

"How much cash do you have left?"

"I don't know. What difference does it make?"

"If you have the money and you still want to see your brother, why not fly to Ireland yourself?"

Ari scratched his wolverine sideburns.

"I suppose I could do that. What's another seven hundred dollars in the long run? And I could give you the concert tickets, so they don't go to waste."

"You could take Hailey too. Why don't you?"

"I don't know about taking Hailey. She'd feel left out. Jeremy and I need time to ourselves."

"Oh come on. Hailey would love Ireland. There are castles, the ocean, and great music. I've been there. It's beautiful. Hailey's a cool girl. She won't get bored."

"She's working two jobs, Myles. She doesn't have money for a trip to Ireland right now."

"I thought maybe you'd treat her. Murphy will give you an advance."

"Jesus Christ you don't know when to stop, do you? I'm already in this one ticket too many. Now you want me to pay for two more? Reality, Myles. Never been your strong suit."

"Screw taking Hailey then. Just you go. All I'm saying is, I think you could use a trip."

Ari yawned. He wanted me to let the subject go, and I couldn't convince him to stay for another round. I walked him to the subway. Ari said he'd let me know about the concert tickets. Then he thanked me for taking on the writing position with Murphy. "Don't give up," he said. "You're doing a good job. Ethan's a hard guy to crack."

I thanked him for his encouragement and watched him duck underground to the subway. Somehow I knew it would be a long time before we'd see each other again, and that everything would change in the interim. A week later a package came for me bearing the concert tickets and one of Jeremy's CD's. Ari had bought that plane ticket to see his brother after all.

10:47 P.M., Wednesday, March 5, 2008

Ethan's interrogation methods were not the stuff of Abu Ghraib, thank God, but they were ridiculous. Jim and Sam were terrified. They both lay stretched out on the ground, their necks strained. Sam had a black and blue cut on his forehead where Ethan head-butted him. He held out a weak hand and begged Ethan to stop ripping pages out of their passports.

"Jesus, man. You don't know what you're doing!" Sam cried as Ethan used a pocketknife to slit his passport photo and bar code page into strips the size of negatives. Jim, meanwhile, suffered more from the sight of all that money slipping away.

Ethan ordered me to count the cash out loud. I counted the hundreds first, then the stacks of fifties. There were small bills too—ones and fives—and for good luck, a small envelope with two-dollar bills.

"What? You thought you needed luck? You had no idea," Ethan said, seizing every opportunity to taunt the traitors.

A Meeting Without Ari
(September 2007)

"Yes, lads, be angry at your parents. 'Tis fine and fair to feel anger," Murphy said, beginning his address. The group was preparing for a morning protest in front of the UN. Everyone was in good cheer. They wore buttons, repeated slogans and took turns throwing darts at a poster of President Bush. As soon as Murphy raised his voice, applause punctuated by the ex-Marines' big "Hoo-rahs!" filled the room. They called for toasts, tapping spoons against whiskey glasses and crowding around the podium.

"'Tis ironic. You're the privileged generation, aren't you? You're the blessed American generation that travels and texts—spoiled brats who don't know a thing about hard work. So I've heard, but I don't believe. What privilege? Boys, I put it to you plain: Your parents are cowards, hypocrites. A greedy lot they are. They betray you. Ask yourselves, what privileges have they bestowed besides their incompetent leadership?"

The old man paced before us, preaching fire and brimstone. The lights dimmed. His voice leapt octaves. My heart beat fast. Murphy was convincing.

"My friends, the ruling generation—your parents—has spent recklessly, governed foolishly, drained resources and squandered our good spirit. Their lot disgusts me. They've stolen their own children's future. Now they've used words like 'duty' and 'honor' and shown you pictures of our burning towers to stir up your emotions and justify sending you off to war. You were all like the Kaiser's men in the beginning, weren't you? Vulnerable creatures of humility—honest patriots sent to fight an imperialist war."

Murphy pounded the podium. His face seared red. "Damn the generation that asked this of you. I see the pictures of torture and bloodshed, the dead coming home in body bags and the boys who have lost their limbs. Mistakes were made at Abu Ghraib. Occupation has left scars. I'm not surprised. We should expect cruelty from poor lads sent to fight a war they cannot possibly understand. And here at home we shun the heroes who stood together on the battlefield so that we can hide our shame for having erred."

"Now that you're home from the wars, take a good long look around at this dying capitalism and ask, who owns the means? Whoever controls the economy bears the responsibility for brokering an honorable end to this war."

"Our parents do!" Lee shouted in response to Murphy's rhetorical question.

"Yes, a sad truth. Only one generation at a time rules the day. You'll have your turn, now your parents are in charge. But why send you to war in the first place? 'Tis not *your* war. This will never be your war. 'Tis theirs. This war is your parent's inevitable oil war, brought on by the burden of '*you*,' or so they say, in their condescending tone." With his bony hand, Murphy indicated us, all the young men in the room—our parent's children. "Considerations for your future weigh heavily on your parent's minds. They have greedily consumed and hoarded resources, believing they were providing for their offspring. Now, the baby boom generation chases the antiquated American dream of *their* parents, but this ideology is utterly bankrupt."

"'Tis as if you're to be sorry for your own birth. Oh, cruel mum and dad. They've gone and measured your entitlement on their scale of crooked values. Your entitlement is their burden. That's what they'd have you believe, and `twas all it took to justify sending their boys off to war to fight and die for their bloody comforts, their status quo. They sent you off to school or to war to become like them, pathetic pawns of capital. Now your debt ensures your servitude."

"Yes, lads, be angry. Never before has the poor world witnessed such a crime. `Twas trickery to say there were Weapons of Mass Destruction. `Twas propaganda to say Saddam Hussein was a madman. Now that you're all home from the wars, ask yourselves what good you did over there, shooting Arabs in the desert? The government may be corrupt, but `tis your parents who endorse its policies with their apathy."

"Perhaps, you think, we should retreat a tad in our argument. 'They're our parents after all. Mustn't we respect them?' Yes, offer respect, but don't be afraid to confront their faults. Let us, for example, consider the extraordinary corruption of this country's wealthy and the acquiescence of the middle class. My friends, no country on earth can keep up with the needs of today's upper classes—a spoiled, consumer generation. They are greed driven maniacs. They built an unlikely empire and justified their course in Iraq by pretending to defend human rights. But we see through the scrim, don't we lads? Your parents merely pledged their sons and daughters to fight in their stead when it came to defending their luxuries and property."

"Yes, blame your parents. They've blood on their hands. A greedy middle class, determined to leap to riches, demanded a fool's revenge for 9/11. `Twas their capitalism, their gas guzzling cars, vacation homes and luxuries that sent them singing *'support the troops!'* 'Twas your parent's debts that necessitated your sacrifice."

"Shall we fiddle while Rome burns? We may be too late. The die has been cast, the damage done. Our leaders warn: 'Beware the mounting debt.' They say that, and the dollar somersaults at your expense. Freedom *isn't* free, but war is too expensive. Mark me words, boys, Iraq will bring the country to its knees. If we do not interfere, your parents will be bankrupted, your inheritance squandered. We must pledge ourselves to a path of honor. We must inaugurate a new and irresistible revolution. Tomorrow, therefore, when you march upon the United Nations and condemn the puppet president, think of all the revolutions that precede yours. Think of the energies that must combine to make progress possible. Ask: must we be brutal?"

"I say, if brutality prompts men to act upon their better instincts, then the ends *will* justify the means. We must close our ears to those who advise against the rising pitch of our protest, those who seek to pacify our ardor through *'quiet debate.'* I fought for my principles in Ireland and I am prepared to fight with the same passion here. I am even ready to give me life for this cause. There, boys, is the recipe for change. An unflinching hand led by an unflinching heart!"

"Yes the brutalities of progress will be called revolutions," he quoted someone as he closed, "when they are over, men recognize that the human race has been harshly treated, but also that it has moved forward. Revolution? What is so terrifying about that word? Are we to be intimidated by the concept of change?"

"No!" the boys cheered.

One last time Murphy's voice turned to thunder. "Yes, blame your parents!" he roared, waving his fist in the air. "When we set out for tomorrow's protest, remember, lads: Remember all the years and the friends your parents stole from you. Remember that you were asked to give up everything to save them their comforts. Show your parents how they've failed you, how they've used you. Expose their waste. Mob the UN tomorrow. Stop the President's car. Interrupt their conference. Let the country and the world know that your generation has a soul!"

Murphy had sent us soaring. The boys swarmed their professor, cheering, whistling and reaching out to shake his hand. His speech still echoed when the music started again. I watched Chris and Lee mumble angry phrases under their breath as though they were practicing for an argument with their parents.

In conversation, everyone moaned about the cruelty of "the system" and the injustices of the war. I caught up with Alan in the kitchen. He'd worked himself into a fit.

"Professor's right, you know?" Alan said. Still dressed up from work, he was pulling uncomfortably at his tie and rubbing under his glasses. I let him vent a Big Echo monologue: "I'm going to confront my dad," he swore vengeance. "I always thought that's the *dream*, do better than you're old man. But that's impossible. I'm $80,000 in debt from school. I can't even get started. The best job I can get barely lets me live in New York without Murphy's help. I'm sick of begging, and it's my dad's fault. He didn't give me a choice, pushed me to be Ivy League all my life. I'll never pay that money back, Myles. School wasn't worth that much. My dad would kill me if he knew about our meetings here, but I don't care. Not anymore."

Ethan swung the closet door open interrupting his rant. Frida was hiding inside with Josie. Nat would have loved their joke. Dressed in flashy red dresses, they stepped out and pretended to be Bob Barker's game-show girls. We all laughed when they took turns stretching out their arms to show off the orange, "Gitmo" prison costume that Ethan had bought at a thrift shop.

"Tomorrow, you'll go to the protest in style!" Ethan announced, playing host. "These practical yet trendy designs can be seen from a mile away. You'll never be cold again in this jump suit—all at the expense of the American taxpayer. Sorry folks, no shoelace draw strings on the hoodie, that's a suicide risk. We can't have prisoners chasing martyrdom and virgins."

Ethan kept going until he and Josie fell on the couch laughing. Then Frida chased Dylan down for a hug.

"You look fancy," Dylan said, his hand resting on her hips.

"Let's go somewhere?" Frida said, kissing him on the cheek.

"Soon," Dylan whispered. Something in Murphy's speech had made him uncomfortable. He sought an excuse to leave.

When I turned around, Landon was taking song requests for his playlist. I requested a song by Wilco, then made my way to the other room.

Near the piano, Sam and Jim were smoking cigars with Professor Murphy.

"Look, Bernie, there's no problem. We've got everything covered," Sam said. I was always surprised when someone got away with calling Murphy by a nickname. Jim was nearly as irreverent, often calling the professor "Bernard."

"Jim has set aside two hundred thousand," Sam continued, draping his arm over Murphy's shoulder. "That should be enough to bail everyone out. I'm taking the day off. I'll hang around the courthouse in case the cops make any arrests. Got to support the troops!"

Jim looked like a fat party boss with a cigar wedged between his too-white teeth. Gobs of gray smoke spilled out of his mouth and he laughed when Professor Murphy wriggled out from under Sam's arm.

"You think I'm worried, aye?" Murphy said, annoyed. "I'm not worried at all. I know you'll do fine if there's to be any trouble with the cops. We've enough quid handy to have our way in this. I only wish Ari was here. He'd keep our boys in check. You know how rowdy Ethan and Landon can be."

"Did I hear my name?" Landon said, stepping into the conversation. He must have taken something. I'd never seen him act so loose. Hard as I'd tried to arrange an interview with Landon, he was the only one in the group who managed to avoid me at every turn. I would have rather heard the story from the man himself, but Dylan provided sufficient summary. Landon's scars were from a roadside bomb that exploded when he was patrolling a Baghdad market. If that wasn't bad enough, his wife cheated on him while he was abroad. Supposedly, she'd spent his entire hazard pay arranging a divorce lawyer while he recuperated at Landstuhl Medical Center in Germany. Recently, he'd been diagnosed bipolar.

Perhaps Landon's condition explained his extreme tastes in music. He insisted on being the DJ at every party and would always confuse the mood, alternating between scores of gangster rap, heavy metal and classical sonatas. As far as I could tell, he hated my indie music requests. Sure enough, he cut my Wilco song short so that he could play a Beethoven symphony.

"What the hell is this?" Sam asked.

Landon rattled off a sophisticated answer. He was a regular Wikipedia entry when it came to remembering the details of the 'Beast' composer's life. Then he closed his eyes and waved his hands like a maestro—his whole body in tune with the dramatic music.

"Man," he said, opening his eyes again and revealing dilated pupils. "When I was on bed-rest in Germany they played smooth classics like this on the radio every morning. I was addicted. You've got to undo the brainwash of that army metal-adrenaline somehow. Know what I mean? I like to play a soft one and then a hard one...."

"You going to wear one of those sporty Gitmo costumes tomorrow?" Jim asked Landon.

"Fuck no. That's Ethan's show."

"When will Bush address the General Assembly?"

"9 o'clock, I think," Landon answered. "Did you hear Chris' idea?"

We shook our heads and leaned in to hear him speak over the thundering piano music.

"We've got tons of Abu Ghraib footage and we're mounting TV's on wheels. We'll play the video as we march uptown."

Jim and Sam were intrigued, but Professor Murphy said little. Suddenly, he passed his cigar to Landon and excused himself. When he was out of sight, Jim started laughing.

"He's nervous. I can't believe the old bloke's got jitters."

"I'm going to smoke this outside," Landon said, pointing toward the balcony. "Anyone coming with?"

I followed Landon out. On the fire escape stairs, everyone was huddled close, puffing smoke and playing Big Echo. I joined in the game, receiving the topic, "Apples." Dylan performed one on travel. Frida spoke about her love of decorative candles, and Lee got sentimental when he chose the prompt "brotherhood." Then Landon blew us all away with his story of the strip-club he'd gone to the first night he was home from the war.

"I was a broken man when I got back, right? I had these scars. I had that bitch of a wife I wanted to kill. No job. Nothing! That's rock bottom for you, but me, I don't care. You know what I do? I go to Big Momma's—way out in Queens. Had to take a taxi both ways. I only wanted to see some boobies, you know? Finally, some ripe, black boobies like I'd been craving. I spent my whole savings in one night—$2,000. When I'm on a binge I never count my money. I withdraw the max and spend till I hit red. I kept buying them hoochies drinks, ordering up dances, slipping ones in their panties. Best goddamn binge of my life. When I'm good and hot, one chick takes me out back to offer up the goodies. I was ready to go, had my pants down and everything. Then this big bouncer whispers the price in my ear. Jesus Christ! They wanted five grand for a fuck. No discount for veterans. I had to get out of there. It's bright morning when I stumble outside, my clothes all messed. I had no idea I'd been there all night."

Suddenly, Ethan pressed his cheek up against the window, startling everyone. He looked ridiculous dressed in that Gitmo costume, and dragging Josie along by the arm. The poor girl was embarrassed. I helped them climb out to the fire escape. In the crisp fall air, Josie's nipples were hard dots on her chest. Drunken Ethan couldn't stop staring. When he saw me looking too, he got angry.

"What the hell is this?" he yelled.

"Nothin.' We's just smoking' this-n-that, havin' us some fun," Landon answered for me.

"We need to talk, Myles," Ethan said, stabbing a hard finger into my chest. He hung his arm over my shoulder and pointed down the thin metal walkway that hugged the façade. "Walk the plank," he demanded.

I started. Ethan followed. He didn't say anything until he was sure nobody could hear us.

"Where's Ari, Myles? We know he told you."

"What the hell?"

"Ari was supposed to march with us tomorrow. He had a responsibility, but nobody has heard anything from him for three weeks."

"What makes you think I have any idea where he is? Why don't you ask his girlfriend?"

"We tried. She's missing too. Come on, Myles. You guys are old friends. If he went somewhere, he'd tell you."

"No, he wouldn't. Ethan, no offence, but you don't know a thing about me and Ari."

Now I was worried. Three weeks *was* a long time. What could have happened to Ari? On the other hand, I was pleased they couldn't find Hailey either. Ari probably decided to invite her on the trip.

"When was the last time you saw him?" Ethan grilled.

"Here, in the afternoon. That same day you and I went out," I said, neglecting to mention how Ari and I had met up later that night at the bar.

"And he didn't say anything?"

"Nothing. He said he couldn't talk. He was headed uptown with Professor Murphy. Landon was there too. He'll vouch for me. Ethan, this is ridiculous. Ari and I were friends in college. We've barely seen each other since the summer. I'm busy. He's busy. This is New York. Everybody's busy."

"Fucking traitor," Ethan fumed. I couldn't tell who he was talking about.

"Ethan, you're drunk. I'll call Ari tomorrow. Promise."

My arms went limp when Ethan grabbed me by the shirt. "Fuck you," he said.

I turned my head to avoid the spray of his slurs. He shook me, demanding I tell him where Ari was. I experienced vertigo, looking down. My back was against the banister. I felt the rickety metal stairs shake beneath me. Everyone was staring.

"Ethan, no!" Josie yelled, rushing to my rescue. "Let him go."

"He knows where Ari is," Ethan said. "But he won't tell."
I shook my head at her, insisting I had no idea.

"Baby, let him go. He doesn't know."

Some of the rage went out of Ethan's eyes as Josie rubbed his back and whispered soothing words in his ear. Then my feet touched the ground again. Ethan didn't say anything, but he let me go and brushed me off.

"Are you ok, Myles?" Josie asked.

I told her I was fine and took a breath.

"Ethan, baby. Maybe we better go back inside and get you some water?" Josie suggested.

Ethan shook his head. "No. Leave me alone. I need to talk to Myles a little longer. I won't grab him again. I promise."

The beast was tamed. Everyone started clapping for us as Ethan and I shook hands and made up.

"Close call, huh Myles?" Lee called from the stairs.

"No," Josie insisted. "Ethan wasn't going to hurt him."

The situation averted, Josie cautiously returned to the Big Echo game, leaving me at the end of the platform with Ethan.

"I don't understand. Why would Ari run off like that? He's the brains behind all our plans," Ethan explained. "That's why I'm angry. Ari abandoned us. We've been planning the protest tomorrow forever, and now he's not even going to show up? Fuck him. Fuck the war. Fuck this whole fucking city."

"Ethan, don't worry. Tomorrow will go fine," I promised, rambling. "I don't know where Ari is, but I'm sure he didn't mean to let you down. Something probably came up. Right? Why don't you try giving him another call."

But Ethan wasn't listening anymore. He was staring wide-eyed into Mydilda's bedroom. "Jesus Christ," he uttered, almost drooling. "That bitch is beating the bush!"

10:55 P.M., Wednesday, March 5, 2008

Landon was quiet. Creepy quiet. He'd entered the apartment through the fire escape. By the time we realized he was watching us, he had us all under his gun.

Ethan put his hands up and slowly stood back from Jim and Sam. As soon as they were free, they scuttled backward to the wall with the mural.

"Thank God, it's you, Lando. Ethan's gone mad. Look what he's done," Sam said, wiping blood from his face.

Unmoved, Landon peered through the sight on his sniper rifle, pinning me, then Ethan, then the two clowns whimpering on the floor. He didn't look as though he gave a damn which of us died first.

"Landon?" Jim asked. "Lando, say something, will you?"

A Meeting Without Ari
(September 2007, Continued)

Ethan grabbed one of Professor Murphy's golf clubs and a pair of binoculars before he led the charge up to the roof.

"I bet everyone in the whole lonely city is polishing the knob with the blinds open," he promised. The rest of us were out of breath, chasing after him on the stairs. At the top, he burst through the heavy door, into the night. Then he began hollering sloppy verses of his new song, "Watching Mydilda." Wild Lee and Landon sang along.

Sure enough, once we were gathered upstairs, searching the skyline, free porn popped up everywhere. One girl was taking a shower across the street. A guy was jerking it from the 15th floor of a high-rise. Below, a young couple had returned from a date. They were busy undressing each other.

Alan tried to remind Ethan that Josie was at the party.

"She doesn't mind. She knows I'm joking," Ethan said, refusing to show embarrassment. When Josie begged Ethan to calm down, he grabbed her breast.

"Baby, you're hurting me!" she shrieked. Laughing, he let her go. She ran and buried her head in my chest.

Ethan was out of control. One minute he was bouncing up and down in his Gitmo jump suit, singing. The next, he was recklessly swinging that golf club around and yelling curses about the army. I knew Josie was terrified, but I was reluctant to interfere. Josie treasured her role as Ethan's caretaker, and he depended on her good heart.

"Last time he got this way he peed on me," Josie explained. "He didn't mean to. We were in bed, and he had a bad dream. Ethan remembers stuff from the war, you know? He doesn't always know where he is when he wakes up."

She wasn't complaining. She was only scared that he'd hurt himself or someone else. Realizing that she had no power to move him, I volunteered to take Ethan back downstairs. I walked steadily toward the soldier but grew nervous when I realized the precariousness of the situation. Ethan was giving a patriotic lecture about New York and saluting an illuminated American flag across the city.

"Where else in the world can you think about hitting a ball down that?" he hollered, pointing down the blurry, flashing avenue at all the yellow taxis rushing through green lights, the stunning silhouette of midtown, our gloomy Gotham in the distance. "That's what we're fighting for, Goddamn-it. You have to fight to be free!"

God, he was drunk. He was absolutely spoiled with drink. Every time he got close to the edge of the roof a shiver ran down my spine.

It took almost an hour, and a couple hard falls, but Alan and I finally did manage to get Ethan downstairs. Professor Murphy glared at us and pointed toward his office. "Put him on the sofa," he ordered. "Make sure he's got a bucket."

We started dragging Ethan down the hall, but then he was sick. Luckily the bathroom was nearby. For the next half hour, Ethan knelt over the toilet, retching. Alan brought him water, and Josie rubbed his back.

11:00 P.M., Wednesday, March 5, 2008

Someone was downstairs making a racket. He'd stubbed his toe and was swearing loudly. Then he began mocking Murphy's accent. "Your fecking pissed, aren't you, lad?" he laughed, "lad, lad, laddie?"

Nobody moved. We were dead quiet. Jim and Sam stared up at Landon, who still controlled the room with his rifle. Landon produced a pistol from the inside pocket of his bulletproof vest and moved stealthily across the floor. At the door, he peeked through the peephole. Then he crept backwards, his eyes reflecting despair.

"It's a lost cause," he mumbled.

Now Landon retreated as stealthily as he'd entered the apartment. On his way out of the room, he disarmed Ethan and collected up the other guns that were scattered about. He didn't know I still had my Luger.

"For fuck's sake, light. Will you?" The drunk in the hall struggled to ignite a match. Finally, we smelled his cigarette under the door. Landon crept backward toward the fire escape.

Faster than Dillinger hitting a bank, he packed all the guns and a few stacks of Jim's money away in a black duffel bag. Then he slipped out the window, vanishing into the night.

Now, the drunken fool barged in. Of all people, it was Alan, laughing like the Joker.

"What the feck is this?" he said, mixing up accents. "What a feckin' joke. You're all here? Howdy, cowards. Howdy-do! Ethan, my God, I'm surprised to see you. I didn't figure you'd be in this bunch. I thought you'd fire the first shot… I saw Ari and Dylan walk off. I saw Lee leave, too. That was predictable." Alan smoked, exhaled and pointed to Jim and Sam. "I never expected these two clowns to show up, they should have skipped town long ago." Then he turned back to Ethan and me. "Hey, what the hell are we doing?" he asked. "It's past 10:30. If the bomb went off, there should be news."

Ethan wanted to sock Alan, but he was more eager to find out if anything had happened. He turned on the television and channel surfed.

There was nothing.

"You smell rotten," I told Alan. He grinned, waved his whiskey flask and took a swig.

"Here's to the end of the world, boys," Alan joked. Then he noticed Sam gathering scattered bills into his pockets and all the dried blood on our clothes.

"Murphy wasn't here, was he?" he asked. "Did he rough you up? Boy, we're in trouble. I checked. Murphy wasn't at his post."

A Meeting Without Ari
(September 2007, Continued)

While Alan and Josie were in the bathroom taking care of Ethan, I found myself looking up at that graffiti mural. Themes were beginning to evolve, and Chris had done a lot of promising work around the edges. He was standing nearby.

"Did you draw this?" I asked, pointing to the corner where someone had pictured a tarantula climbing up a yellow street lamp. Chris came closer, a crayon in hand. He knelt down, added a few dots of black here and there and gave each line a careful smudge to blend the colors.

"The mural has a concept now," he said. "You know that spider web tattoo Landon has on his arm?" I didn't remember, so Chris pointed him out in the corner. Landon was crashing from his high. He sat on the floor with his eyes closed and his headphones on. His sleeves were rolled up and I could see the lines drawn around his elbow.

"Ethan has one, too," Chris said. "Each ring of the web stands for an insurgent they killed in Iraq. Landon rarely speaks unless he's stoned, but when he does, it's poetry. Beautiful stuff—that image. No offense, Myles. You're a decent writer, but I doubt if you could do better than that for a symbol."

"I'm not a poet," I said, defending my writing.

Chris didn't care. "For a soldier who kills, the spider web becomes a metaphor for life and death," he explained "The bigger it grows the more lives he's caught. But even the master of the web knows his life is fragile. A fierce wind will blow him away."

I thought Chris was talking straight out of his ass, but I let him have his moment. After all, I liked his picture.

"Do you plan to connect all the mural scenes with a spider web?" I asked, trying to get a sense of the drawing's direction.

Chris nodded. Then he searched the mural as though it were a map for all his thoughts. "You don't realize how soothing drawing is until you start," he said. "That's what this mural is. This is a space for free speech. The boys experiment, and I do all the web work. A lot of them think they make mistakes when it comes to drawing, so I show them how to fix their work. You can always fix a picture. It's a therapy we're developing."

As I retreated down the hall to check on Ethan, I watched Chris draw red lines, then color in a patch of blue. When he added a smudge of white, the sketch revealed the contours of a battle torn American flag.

# 11:10 P.M., Wednesday, March 5, 2008

"You do know there is a live Webcam for Time Square?" Alan said, starting up his laptop. His hipster ironies and attitude were too much. Ethan's temper flared.

"That's enough out of you," he growled, commandeering the computer. Soon there was an image of the Army recruiting station on the screen, but no sign of anyone from our group.

Then my phone rang.

"Myles? Hurry. Leave the apartment."

"Dylan?" I asked. The connection was poor. He was calling from a payphone.

"Murphy killed him. He's following me."

"Dylan, slow down. Where are you?"

"Will you fucking shut up and listen to me? I'm downtown. Where else? If you're still at the apartment, get out. Now!"

Dylan was panting. "Murphy pushed him," he cried.

"Pushed who?"

"Chris. He's in the alley between 34th and 35th. Murphy threw him off the roof."

"You're making that up. I just saw Chris."

"Why would I make that up? I saw him fall with my own fucking eyes. Chris didn't stand a chance. Murphy came out of nowhere. He killed him, Myles. He'll kill you too. Get the hell out of that apartment! Get out of the city…"

Sirens. Static. I was losing the call. "Ok. I'm leaving. Can you hear me? I'm leaving now," I yelled into the phone, but Dylan was gone.

I hung up. The room was silent. Everyone was staring at me.

"Chris?" Ethan said the name he'd overheard. "Is he dead?"

A Meeting Without Ari

(September 2007, Continued)

Somehow, Ethan recovered. Now Josie, Alan and I sat with him in Professor Murphy's study. Alan passed around his laptop, and a fat joint.

"It's a YouTube jukebox party!" Josie said, as we took turns searching classic songs on the Internet. The game was fun. We swore we'd stay up all night and never get tired.

"The 90's were unreal," Josie theorized, resting her head on Ethan's shoulder and playing with his blonde hair. Her sweet nostalgic monologue came in response to a Silver Bullet Band song. "That wealth was all an illusion," she suggested. "We were duped into believing we were happy and secure. People think we lost something when the planes hit, but the truth is our prosperity was never real."

She got dreamy in the smoke. As soon as her voice faded, Ethan went on the offensive:

"Josie-girl, you're out of your mind," he said. "You talk like somebody who never went up in the towers." When he saw Josie frown, he grew worried. "Seriously? Don't tell me now that you never went up there?"

"You mean *the* towers,'" Josie stung back, sticking out her tongue.

"Jesus, I can't believe this. My own girl doesn't even know why I went to war. That's a story for you, Myles. Write that down. It says something about the public disconnect. Josie, if you smelled the burning jet fuel that day, I know you'd remember things differently. I was there. I saw the towers collapse. I breathed their dust. Jesus, you all don't know what you missed. My dad took me up there once when I was a kid. When you rode the elevator all the way to the top, that was something else. If you're telling me that all those skyscrapers, bridges, roads and homes that you can see from up that high don't add up to a lot of wealth that's real, then shit. I don't know what to tell you. Tell me you went up there, Josie. Tell me you saw the Towers before they fell?"

Alan grinned, watching them argue. "Myles, you pick one," he said, passing me the computer. I chose an Israeli song, changing the mood.

"Do you reckon the wars all stem from Palestine?" I asked the group.

Ethan thought Arabs. Alan thought Jews. Josie thought oil.

"You know, we were damn close. Would have been nice to meet when I had furlough," Ethan said, remembering I'd been in Israel while he was still on active duty. "I mean it's the 'Middle East,' for crying out loud. The most contested real estate on the planet. And you Jews, of all people, have to own the place."

"How about Myles and I make the Jewish jokes?" Alan said wanting Ethan to dial back the intensity of his comments. Alan always exposed Zionist sensitivities whenever anyone called him out for being a Jew.

"I don't like this music. Change the song?" Josie said, playing diplomat.

I passed her the computer. Josie searched indecisively, and then put on a Beatles song.

"Did you guys see that writing on the wall?"

"You mean the, 'Do We Still Believe The Beatles' sign?"

"Who wrote that?" Josie asked, her bloodshot eyes squinting in the smoke.

Ethan stood up. He walked out of the room, still shivering from having been sick. When he returned, he looked refreshed. "I left a check under: No!" he said, proudly announcing his discouraged opinion of the British band. "Lennon was a phony."

Next, Ethan wandered toward Professor Murphy's bookshelf. There was a stack of board games on the top rung, including Chess, Parcheesi and Risk.

"Let's conquer the world!" Ethan said, grabbing Risk off the shelf. We all agreed to play, but of course the game took too long to set up. The more cards we drew and the more armies we placed, the sleepier Ethan and Josie became. Finally, they both passed out on the sofa. Alan helped me cover them up with a blanket. Then we sat down on the floor and put our backs against Professor Murphy's desk. Alan rubbed his eyes under his square glasses, and I raided the desk-drawer liquor stash that Murphy had revealed during my interview, choosing a little glass jug of Arrack.

"That's what they drink in Israel, isn't it?" Alan asked.

"Yes," I answered. "Do you still have ice in your glass?"

Alan had two small cubes left from a whiskey. We split them up and poured a clear shot over each. Within seconds, a milky white cloud appeared around the ice. Alan proposed a toast to the Jewish homeland. I laughed and sipped the bitter anise. Immediately, I felt flushed and feverish.

"Alan, I don't get it," I asked the question that had been bothering me all night. "What's going on here? Why are guys like Jim and Sam supporting our group? They practically contradict everything Murphy said tonight"

"I suppose they feel guilty. Sam lost a friend in Iraq. Jim is his buddy. They got involved. So what?"

"Then what the hell are *we* doing here? We're not soldiers."

"We're doing what's right. The war is awful. Don't you agree? The whole system is wrong, and we've got to make a stand."

"Alan, wake up. We're hardly organized. You really think attending tomorrow's protest will accomplish anything? This war will go on a long time, whether we like it or not."

"You're the last person I expected to hear say something so defeatist. You've changed. Weren't you always trying to get me and Ari to come to socialist meetings in college?"

"I was going through a phase. Besides, this is different," I said, hoping to disarm him. Clearly, Alan was disappointed in me. He thought I didn't sense the bigger picture.

Alan had another joint in his pocket. He sighed and undid his tie. Then he lit up and took a long drag before handing it to me. I held the smoke in my lungs until I began to sweat.

"I don't know, Myles. You've got to believe in *something*, don't you?" Alan said. He had a hole in his pant leg from when he tripped, dragging Ethan downstairs. His finger found the hole, and he played incessantly. "Something bad is coming. I'm certain. A couple of years ago, when you, me and Ari used to do this kind of thing in college—smoke and talk—we were never pessimistic like this, were we? Man, we'd do some scheming. Josie's right. That was still the 90's for crying out loud. We were going to make big money, and it was all a game. That's not so easy anymore. The rules changed after 9/11, and now we've lost our way."

Finally, Alan admitted to me what was really eating him. "They're going to sack me at work," he predicted. "There's nothing I can do."

We stared at each other. I didn't know what to say. Everybody I knew in the city was going through the same thing, and I could feel my optimism fading too. Good thing Ethan was snoring. That provided a distraction. We watched Josie rise and fall across Ethan's back as he breathed heavily. Then I tried to reposition Ethan's head on the pillow to quiet him down.

"Anyway, do you want to know how I see it going down?" Alan asked when I returned to my seat on the floor.

"See what go down?"

"The grand finale. The big blow out war with Iran and China and the end of capitalism. Israel gets a few licks in, by the way. They're essential to the final conflict."

I pointed to the Risk board and all the different colored pieces we'd spilled out across the map of the world.

"Show me?"

Alan chose red for China. He dropped a big pile of armies in the Gobi Desert and explained how the nation would need to expand in all directions.

"There's too many people. Not enough resources. There will be a war with Russia before they take us on."

I nodded, waiting for him to continue.

"But the real powder keg is here," he said, carefully placing different colored pieces in the Middle East. "Europe is a bad ally. They're hiding under our nuclear umbrella while they attend therapy sessions to ease their Holocaust guilt. They play both sides when they want cheap oil, and then they screw us over when we need their help."

Alan paused to hit the joint and tidy up some of the pieces. "That's where we come in," he said, grinning as he picked out a pile of green figurines to represent the "good guys." The more he elaborated on the details of his war game, the more animated he became.

"The US is the only country with an army capable of seizing the oil. For us, the job looks plain and simple. We've got to control the oil fields before the Chinese buy everything in sight. But we get tied up because our bullshit allies—the Europeans—are cowards, and it's politically incorrect to be imperialist."

"Look here," he said, drawing an imaginary circle around Tehran and Jerusalem. "The fighting starts in Israel, of course. I mean those guys are practically begging to get off our leash. If the Americans would let them, they'd fly their whole air force over to A-mena, A-mena, oh fuck, I can never say his name, 'I'm-a-nut-job's' palace today, and blow him off the face of the earth."

"Mahmoud Ahmadinejad," I said, laughing.

"Right. Anyway, Americans want to fight Iran, but we're too war weary from this mess in Iraq and Afghanistan. We've got some ammunition left, but nobody has any stomach to pick another fight. Someone else has to deal the first blow. That's why we let the Israelis get in over their heads bombing Iran. That gives us an excuse to come in later and be the heroes who bail everyone out."

"What does China do when we attack?"

"Right! China is where we get our ass kicked. Then it's a meltdown. You can see it happening, can't you?"

"Sure Alan. We're on the brink," I said, shaking my head and laughing.

"Look, Myles, I'm going to tell you the same thing that Ari told me when I first got involved here. He said: 'Alan, were grown men. Now we have to decide where we stand on the issues. No more games.'"

"Ari said that?" I asked, almost gagging on my Arrack.

"Sure he did, and he's right. Americans can't be apathetic forever. We have to decide what we want in the world besides oil."

Alan was searching my eyes, searching hard for sincerity. When he saw me squinting, still laughing at his Risk scenario for world war and Ari's sober turns, he put me on the spot.

"Come on, Myles, I'm serious. Where do you stand?"

I ran my hand across the game board, messing the pieces. "Alan, this is silly. Stop being so dramatic," I said. "Of course, I want what you want. Peace on earth. Boom times. I want the allies to be allies and the West to believe in itself again. Everybody wants that. But if you're asking me to agree that world war is inevitable, I can't. That's unthinkable. It's not 1939. Things aren't that bad. They've been a lot worse."

Alan wasn't sure if he liked my answer.

"Suit yourself. Shit, it's late. I'm fading," he said, standing. I followed him out. The hallway and salon were deserted, but there were still some voices in the far room. We shook hands at the door. "Will you march with us tomorrow?" Alan asked.

I said I'd try my best, but couldn't look him in the eye.

"Doesn't sound promising," Alan said.

"I have to work at the restaurant," I lied. "I'll try and come after my shift. Promise."

"Sure," Alan said, letting it go. Then he began fishing in his pocket. I heard keys jingling. "Take a walk with me?"

He put a cigarette to his lips, opened the door and started down the stairs. When he looked back, surprised that I wasn't following, I shook my head.

"Not tonight," I answered. "I think I'll stick around for another drink. I'm waiting for Nathalie to call."

Alan was already at the bottom.

"Figures. I know you, Myles. Always have to go your own way. Don't you? Have fun with the girl."

11:20 P.M., Wednesday, March 5, 2008

They put on their music to beat the war drums. My ears were ringing as Metal madness roared through the apartment.

Ethan barked orders: "Go to Google!" he yelled. "Look up the subway near 34ᵗʰ and fifth. Chris may still be alive. Hurry!"

"I'm not going anywhere with you," Sam shouted.

"What did you say?" Ethan asked, turning toward him.

"I said I'm not following."

Ethan swung hard. Sam spiraled backward. When he stood up, his nose was gushing blood. Then he noticed the gun poking out of Alan's jacket. He reached fast, pushed Alan out of the way, and fired at Ethan.

The first shot knocked Ethan to the ground. The second shot tore off half his face. He was writhing in pain, holding his head as blood streamed between the cracks in his fingers and soaked through his shirt.

"You're not so tough, are you, Ethan? Dishonorably discharged. I know all about that. You're a worthless coward and a fucking drunk!" Sam yelled, waving the gun at us.

Alan and I threw our hands up, begging Sam not to shoot.

"Get the briefcase," Sam told Jim. The two of them scooped up as many bills as they could into their luggage. Sam's nose was still pouring blood all over his hands and shirt as he backed up toward the door. "I'm getting dizzy," he admitted, handing the gun to Jim.

The music kept blaring. Ethan was screaming, but his voice was gone.

"Sorry boys," Jim muttered, backing out the door behind Sam. He had a key, and he locked us in. Alan and I raced to Ethan's side.

Midnight Special

(September 2007)

I knew right away I'd made a mistake sticking around. The party was over. In its wake, empty beer bottles and filthy ashtrays littered the room. Aside from Ethan and Josie sleeping in the back, the apartment felt cold and abandoned.

Someone grabbed my shoulder. My heart skipped a beat. I gasped.

"There he is," Sam said, laughing at my fright. "Bernie told us to take you out tonight."

"Where is Professor Murphy?" I asked, trying to regain my composure.

"You'll see him later," Jim promised, coming out of the other room and dangling a set of keys. "We're supposed to close up shop."

They ushered me to the door, and Sam turned off the lights.

"Where are we going?"

"Out."

"That's not very descriptive," I said, stepping into the hall.

"Hey, Jim, I think the kid is scared."

"Myles, don't be silly. Afraid of me and Sam? That's ridiculous. We're going to have a good time. Professor Murphy always takes care of his boys. Besides, you're all working too hard in this shitty economy. Time to relax. Let us show you the real city."

We got into a cab on First Avenue. "Take us to the Sony Club—" Sam started to tell the cabby, but Jim interrupted, giving his address instead.

"Why are we going there?" I asked.

Jim started laughing. "Ever hear of a suit?" he asked, scowling at my casual dress.

Things were happening fast. I was wedged between them in the back of the cab, thinking I was dead. After a couple blocks, however, they dropped the gangster act and lightened up. Now they argued about high-end restaurants and fancy call girls, competitively listing the top ten things they loved about New York.

Finally, we stopped in front of Jim's apartment building. The doorman helped us out of the car and said a well-tipped sounding, "G'evening Mister Jim.'" I thought I was back in Vegas on a gambling spree with Ari and Dylan, the way we rushed through the revolving doors into a gold-decorated lobby. My footsteps echoed on the hard, green and white, swirl marble floor.

We sped up to the penthouse in the elevator. Jim typed a code into the panel, and the doors opened up to his incredible view of the city. The space was massive. Jim said all of his furniture was custom designed—made from exotic animals. He had a maid. Everything was neat, tidy and static. In the bedroom, he showed us his vast closet and his most prized possession; a genuine Chagall painting that he'd hung above his king, claw-footed bed.

"That's the thing about great wealth," Sam lectured as I put on dress shoes and tried different blazers. "At some point you *have* to show taste."

I understood that I wasn't going anywhere until they were satisfied with my appearance.

"Try the gray jacket," Jim said. "It's a bit vintage but that will suit Myles. Besides, that's the smallest one."

I pushed my arms through the sleeves and straightened the lapel. The jacket fit decently enough. Black buttons, snug around my shoulders, sleek on the sides.

"Are we ready?" I asked.

Jim looked me over. "Funny," he said, smiling. "The last time I wore that was when I went to interview at Bear Stearns. That was the only jacket I owned. My signing bonus bought me a whole new wardrobe. That was nineteen years ago."

"He needs a tie," Sam said.

"Come on, he doesn't need a tie," Jim argued.

"He looks ridiculous without one," Sam persisted.

"Fine, you pick one out. I'm going to see the doctor." Sam sighed and waved Jim away.

"Who's the doctor?" I asked as soon as Jim was gone.

"Doctor Phil."

"You mean the talk show host?"

This made Sam laugh. Apparently a physician downstairs sold Jim pills.

I was hesitant to try whatever they were popping in the cab.

"What are they?" I asked, fidgeting with the silver tie Jim had lent me.

"Uppers," Jim said, gulping down two of the white pills. Smiling, he quickly handed the bottle to Sam. "They make you feel good."

"One," I said. "Only one."

Sam prescribed two, put his flask in my hand and patted my back hard. Then they waited for me to knock back the capsules.

"That a-boy," they cheered when I finished swallowing.

We got out of the cab at 56th and Madison, in front of the Sony Tower and a window display with flashing digital screens. I followed Jim and Sam through revolving doors, past the tall green atrium and around the corner to the elevators. A porter started to ask us where we were going, but stopped when he recognized the big-shot pair.

"Good evening, Mr. Cohen, Mr. Berkowitz. Going to the club?" he asked, pocketing their twenty-dollar tip and calling the elevator.

The doors opened up into another hallway. At the entrance to the club, ushers took down our names. Beyond the hall, there was a wide foyer that housed a marble staircase surrounded by towering windows. Outside, New York was glowing. I looked across the East River to Queens and imagined I could see the highway leading home to Ithaca.

"Hear that music?" Jim asked. He gave me a nudge and pointed into an adjacent room. "That's your professor playing."

A gentle classical melody filled the air. I wanted to look into the salon, but Jim and Sam were hungry. They pushed me along to the sushi bar at the opposite end of the club. The small room was dark, save for the blue-lit waterfall that trickled down a bamboo-paneled wall.

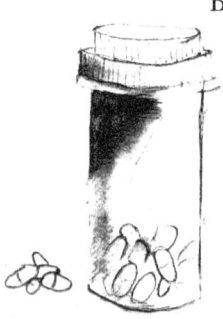

Behind the bar, a round, Asian man with a long face, curlicue beard and a sushi chef's hat leaned over a sleek, black eel. The three of us were mesmerized watching him make swift, steady, dutiful strokes through the fish. The chef wet seaweed in a clay bowl. Next he gently kneaded rice, fish, fruits and vegetables together into rolls.

Suddenly, a slit of light appeared on the back wall, indicating a door. Another small Japanese man emerged carrying a tray of exotic Nigiri. "Mista Burkowit, Mista Cohen. Good to see you. You bring friend? Very good. Here, you try," he said, pointing to a golden, goopy, cut of fish and handing out chopsticks.

"This: sea er-chin. We fly in fresh today. From Japan. You try," he said, watching us struggle to grasp the big pieces with our chopsticks. "Here. Like this. You dip in soy sauce. Put whole thing in mouth. No bites. Chew all at once."

We did as we were told and chewed till the raw fish gushed flavor between our teeth—a light, refreshing taste with a hint of salt, a hint of sweet and the texture of ice cream. Meanwhile, the little man loaded our plates with sushi, sauces and a jug of warm Sake. "Professor play very good tonight. Mr. Murphy very good man. Very generous," he told us repeatedly.

"I fucking love that guy!" Sam said as we sat down to eat in the next room where some men were playing cards and smoking cigars. In the corner, an older woman with shiny, black, wavy hair was looking at me. She crossed her legs, dangling a black pointed shoe from her ankle. Occasionally, she scrolled through emails on her Blackberry.

During intermission, the lounge grew crowded. What a bunch of Gatsby's. Women emerged, dressed in ball gowns and sparkling with diamonds. Clean-shaven men with slick black hair drank champagne and toasted privilege. Meanwhile, that fancy woman in the corner kept eying me every time a waiter rushed past, serving drinks. Then I heard the rattle of Jim's pill bottle again under the table.

"Trust the good doctor!" Sam said, nudging me.

I decided to let go and stop fearing the medicine. What the hell. I felt good. I took some now, and I knew I'd take more whenever the pills were offered.

"Does Professor Murphy know we're here?" I asked.

"Of course," Jim said. "He plays here once a month, and he chooses his audience."

"Why don't the rest of the boys know about this?"

"Because not everyone can afford to get in here, and Professor Murphy told us to keep our mouths shut," Sam said, swallowing a big piece of fish.

"Why did he invite me?"

"Never mind about that. Just try to enjoy. Do you know what tickets cost?" Sam asked.

I shrugged my shoulders.

"A thousand a head."

My jaw dropped.

"Don't worry, we've been comped. But that ought to give you some idea what it takes to run in Bernie's circle. This is the big leagues, Myles. Stick with us. We'll make you king."

I got an idea how their banking empire worked. They'd created a hedge fund that was cashing in on penny exchanges and fluctuations in the turbulent market. The big money, however, was still in real estate. I was desperate to change the subject. They thought they were giving me an education, but I couldn't stand the way they glorified themselves and their aggressive business strategies. They made me feel like such a sucker.

"Who is she?" I said, interrupting.

"No. You'll never," Sam said, dismissing my curiosity about the woman making eyes with me. "That's Mrs. Leonard. Miriam Leonard."

"Ms. Mizzzz!" Jim corrected, remembering the woman's divorce. "She has her stake in Lehman Brothers. Quite the arrangement actually. She made off like a bandit."

"No," Sam disagreed. "That isn't true. She isn't divorced. Something happened to her husband. He disappeared. That's how she wound up with all those shares. Ask Murphy. He knows the whole story."

They told me she was Jewish, that the money was dirty, but that she'd gotten out of the market. Ms. Leonard had cashed in all her chips to become a patron of the arts. "Come to think of it, she owns a small press. That's her baby these days," Sam said, trying to remember the name of the publishing house she had founded.

"A press?" My eyes lit up. In this category, I was as blood-thirsty entrepreneurial as the rest of them.

"Excuse me," I said, getting up. "I want to meet her."

My legs felt unattached, and yet my vision was clear. I seemed to float across the room. Jim and Sam called after me, making a million jokes, but their voices grew distant as I forgot where I was and how I'd gotten there. Soon I blocked them out entirely. When I stood in front of the mystery woman, she asked for my name.

"Miriam," she replied, when I turned the question around. Her voice crackled, emitting a sharp, throaty sound she'd perfected. We shook hands, and when I saw the blue veins that ran down her arm through her dainty wrists, I worried I would squeeze too hard. Her skin was soft and thin and glazed and spotted here and there with, "Florida," she said, explaining the source of her freckled tan.

I asked her where in the Sunshine State, thinking of my Grandfather's winter residence and tried to connect myself to her in a dozen ways. Did she know Cornell? Had she been to Israel? Why was she in New York? But it was hopeless. As far as I could tell, we were separated by at least twenty years, and there was no way our paths could have crossed.

I wasn't sure what about me amused her. I heard our glasses clink. I heard Miriam laugh. I enjoyed her smile. I was thinking that I ought to tell her everything straight away. Tell her about Ari, how he'd gone to Ireland to find his brother, and I was writing the book.

"The novel ends out west. I know that much," I explained as we entered the concert hall and found seats.

Miriam fanned herself with the program and crossed her legs. "Don't tell me too much," she said. "You'll spoil the ending, and I won't want to read a word."

"I'm sorry."

"Don't apologize."

"Sorry."

Awkward and impatient silence followed. Then Miriam had more questions.

"He's going to play Strauss tonight. Do you know your composers?" Miriam asked, pointing at the piano.

I shrugged my shoulders. Where was Landon when I needed him? Luckily, I did have some knowledge of classical music.

"My dad took me to Vienna once," I said. "I was very young but we went to all the tourist concerts where they dress up like Mozart. Have you been there?"

Of course she had. Berlin was her ideal city, however. She said Germany was too proud to cater to American tourists.

"I know," I agreed. "I was there too."

Now she was interested and a tad surprised by the extent of my travels.

"When?"

"Two years ago? Before Israel. I went to Germany for a time."

Miriam combed her hair with her fingers and smoothed her dress. Then came the inevitable question, the one that she had held in reserve up till now as her most powerful means of putting me in my place. "I'm going to age you," she said, laughing. "Tell me the number."

I told her my age. She refused to act surprised.

"How does a kid like you get into a club like this?" she asked.

I looked around for Jim and Sam, but they weren't there. No matter. A lie served me better.

"I'm an usher."

"Where's you're name tag?"

"Long story."

"Is it?"

"I just quit. I was on my way out."

"Nice fib," she said with a smile that seemed to beg for a cigarette. Then she crossed her legs the other way, looked toward the grand piano and laughed a little to herself. Finally, she grabbed my hand.

"Where's your pen, writer?" she asked.

Luckily, I had one on me. Miriam wrote her name and office address on a napkin.

"Bring your manuscript around," she whispered as the lights dimmed and Professor Murphy took his seat at the piano. "I'll be waiting."

11:33 P.M., Wednesday, March 5, 2008

We were going through towels fast, mopping up Ethan's blood. Alan tore off Ethan's shirt so that we could find the bullet hole.

"Thank god the music was playing so loud. I don't think anyone heard the shots," he said, but he was hardly confident. "You don't think anyone heard, do you?"

"Alan, this is New York. If someone heard, the NYPD would be here."

Ethan started to seize and shake uncontrollably. I put a towel in his mouth to prevent him from biting his tongue, and Alan shoved the furniture aside so that his limbs could flail freely. As the convulsions slowed, Ethan's wounds began to seep. Then he lost consciousness.

"We need a doctor," Alan said, watching Ethan's eyes roll back into his head.

"No shit."

"I'll call," Alan said, finding his phone on the card table.

"Don't."

"What?"

"Don't," I repeated, putting my hand out to stop him.

Alan stood up. He was furious with me. "He's going to die," he said.

"Alan, look at him. He's as good as dead."

"No. We have to try. I'm calling for help."

"Don't be a fool. Call 911 and you're going to prison for a long time. Now's our only chance to get away."

"What the hell kind of friend are you? Look at Ethan. He's bleeding to death. I won't let you leave."

Alan started to dial. I backed away.

"Where are you going?" he asked, dropping the call. I didn't reply. I put on my jacket, covering the bloodstains on my shirt.

"What are you planning, Myles?" Alan asked, trying to slow me down.

"Fuck you, Alan. Fuck you both," I lashed out. "What's it look like I'm doing? I'm getting the hell out of here."

I scooped Ari's phone off the table. When I turned around, Alan was barring the door. I reached inside my pocket and grabbed for the Luger. Alan wasn't scared. He threw the TV remote at me, but missed badly.

I charged, hit him across the head with the butt of the pistol and kept kicking him until he rolled out of the way of the door.

Time sped up. I struggled with the lock. Saw the blood red carpet on the twisting stairs. Heard the slamming metal door. Tasted the cool misty air outside. Held my first full breath. Saw the yellow glare of streetlights trickling through alleys and the shadowy smoke stack at the end of the street. I heard the first shrill whine of sirens and the clap of my feet pounding the pavement. I clenched my chest. My heart was throbbing. I was waking up from a bad dream in the middle of the night, and I knew I still had hours of sleepless sleep to sleep.

Crescendo
(September 2007)

*One cone of bright white light encircled Professor Mur-
phy as his fingers fell upon the keys. Hunched like Quasimo-
do, he leaned over the grand piano, his feet tapping the pedals
below, balancing sharps and flats in fluid melody.*

"He's improvising," Miriam whispered. "This crescendo
isn't in the piece."

I didn't answer her. I was dozing.

I clapped when everyone clapped. I stood when everyone
stood. I melted into that crowd surrounding Murphy, praised
him, and wanted to shake his hand.

After the concert, I wandered over to the big marble stairwell and stared out the massive window. Creative
epiphanies electrified my thoughts. Lights squiggled and
streaked across the glass as though I had taken some of
Ethan's DMT. Suddenly, I thought I had the whole book
figured out. I was desperate to be back at my desk where
I could write everything down. But then my reverie was
interrupted.

"A word, Myles?" I felt the pinch of Murphy's bony fingers on my back. He trapped me against the balustrade and
pointed down the flight.

"You've enjoyed yourself, I see?" Murphy said, observing the way I depended on the banister for balance.

"Yes, of course. Thank you for inviting me. Should I keep going?"

We spun around the marble steps more times than I could count. At the bottom, Murphy pushed me down a hall, through a door and into a private study. Then he grabbed me.

"Where is he?" he said, pinning me against the wall, one hand pressing the air out of my chest, the other squeezing my Adam's apple. All pain was delayed.

"Who?" I gasped.

Murphy's hand waved, blurred. I felt a cold wind, then the burning sting of his slap across my cheek.

"Where's Ari!" Murphy growled.

"Fecked if I know," I said, mocking him. I hadn't signed up for this.

He threw me on the floor and kicked me hard in the gut.

"Don't give me any of your lip," Murphy roared, kicking me again with his sharp shoe. "You fecking leech. You know damn well where he is."

Furious tones replaced the quip in his accent. He hissed like a cobra, annunciating every syllable.

"Do you think I pay you for your work? Do you think I give a damn what you write? You're an informer. That's your role. I pay you to keep me boys in check. That's it, and that's all, Myles. Now tell me, where has Ari's gone? Tell me!"

"What makes you think I have any clue where he is?" I cried, astonished that Murphy was in the dark concerning his pupil.

"He's been missing for weeks. Not a word. Just keeps withdrawing money from the account we set up."

"Trace the money yourself. Call the bank. They'll block the card."

I didn't understand why, but that paused Murphy's assault. He stepped away, thinking.

Breathing hard, I pushed my aching back to the wall and tried to stand.

"Who are you?" I asked. "What the hell is going on here?"

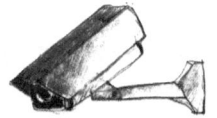

PART II

(Apologies)

Sorry...
I told myself there's time.
But in the hot cold
Bittersweet apocalyptic
No music plays.
True souls slip
As heartbeats skip,
Swift rapids flooding streams.
Dare count their swarm,
Dare dredge their deeps,
Numbness intervenes.
Seed and sod,
Fields of guilt
Feared afar
Contained, confused, unclean.
My lonely friends
All turned around.

12:03 A.M., Thursday, March 6, 2008

Their nostalgic monologues
unraveling: "Years waste
alone, at last, along..."
Desperate, steering clear.
Bewildered Ghosts,
Like deer crossing traffic—
Their bolted legs
upon the road.
Leap:
One last vow-full scream!
Release frightened howls.
Echo crimes with drums
Barking death,
Utter, (their last scene).
Forever headlines
Pulse erratic:
"The shame of sheep,"
The news last week,
Here everyone speaks
Babel in September.

Not fucking poetry. My thoughts were in verse. In cryptic tones, I imagined the morning newspaper headlines:

"Iraq Veteran Found Dead in Alley"
"Embezzled Bank CEO Flees Country"
"Lobbyist & Veteran Wounded in Eastside Gun Battle."
"Terror Group Exposed, Plans Foiled"
"Police Conduct Manhunt For Former IRA Operative."

Drenched in sweat, I stopped running. I was dizzy, too. What street was I on? Was this Harlem already? I dug in my pocket for my lighter and cigarettes. I breathed too deeply on the first drag and started coughing. Still, I smoked it to the stub. Then I threw out the pack. I didn't want the temptation. Besides, I figured Ari and I would buy new later—once I'd found him.

"Time to quit smoking. Time to start eating right. Call home and say sorry!" I was a quotable self-help book, repeating catch phrases, making life-resolutions and hoping to forget my nightmare. Mostly I worried about Ari. Was my friend a murderer? I had to convince myself I'd find him before he made a terrible mistake.

Never had I thought so desperately about people. Suddenly I was sifting through fond memories of everyone involved with the plot. Winter Scenes replayed. I remembered Lee's first piano recital, Ethan's drunken antics and Chris' bitter art. I thought of Alan's apocalyptic slideshows and Dylan's nostalgic talks. I could hear Jim's lectures on philanthropy, Sam's big laugh and Murphy's philosophic intrigues. How could I forget our mood that unseasonably warm November day when Ari, Hailey and I strolled through Central Park? Somehow even Landon's brutish scowl held charms.

Why did Murphy want them dead? What had my friends done to deserve murder? I didn't think they were cowards for having betrayed the Times Square plot.

The novel was the only way I could distract myself. The challenge was to connect every scene and draw out the truth. I didn't know yet if I was running away again, but I'd realized I was finally writing the concluding chapter of my apology. Either Ari would forgive me for what happened with Melissa, or we would never be friends again.

In the Grit of a Binge
(October 2007)

Nice light. The nice light flickered. Warm—th. I crawled off my deflated mattress, climbed toward the light and scribbled notes on the wall.

> "I still have an awful lot to learn about being somebody's brother," Ari told himself as he watched Jeremy drive into the sunset. Ever since they'd set out on the road west, their good-bye at the Canadian border felt inevitable…

I was in character, impulsively writing my novel. Too bad I'd taken too much. I felt ill. Amylase—that too sweet taste flooded my mouth. I gagged and gulped. I couldn't swallow. At last, I spilled my gut into the porcelain bowl. When I returned to my wall, I was a reptile. Cold blood. Papers crinkled. My mind went numb. Asleep, awake, I felt and saw nothing that was real.

"Myles?" Nat said, nudging me. "Myles, wake up! Don't do this to me, ok? Wake up!"

I heard her, but I couldn't move. My back was sore from sleeping on the hard wood floor. Nathalie was too scared to take my pulse. She began to cry when she noticed the ashtray, the beer bottles and the rest of Jim's pills. Her tears dripped on my arm. She didn't know what to do if I was dead. Finally, I managed a breath.

"Myles, thank God. Breathe! Please, keep breathing."

I breathed for her. It made me cough violently. Nat thought I was choking. She slid behind me, propped me up and smacked my back until I hacked up something brown and yellow, all the phlegm coating my lungs. When my cough subsided, I pulled myself to the corner of the room and leaned against the wall. I touched my face; felt the beard-fuzz, the two sore puffballs that were my eyes, my chapped lips and my dried out nose. I had no idea where I'd been, or how long I'd been binging.

"Are you ok?" Nat asked. "Myles, where were you? You've been missing for almost two weeks."

"Are people looking for me?"

"Those friends of yours, Alan and Dylan. Your Mom called. Everyone's worried."

Our apartment came into focus. "I couldn't stay here," I said. "I was scared. I thought he was after me." Nat brought me a wet washcloth to clean my face. I must have fallen because an abrasion on my cheek stung when she touched it with the cloth. "I couldn't call anyone," I continued. "I thought I was in danger."

"Danger?"

"Professor Murphy. He's dangerous," I said, lifting up my shirt to show her the black and blue bruises that had kept me in a state of shock and on the run. Of course, they had all faded.

Nathalie didn't believe a word I said about Ari's eccentric group of veterans, their crazed professor or the Sony Club where I was assaulted. I didn't blame her.

"Myles?" she said, taking a step back. "You wrote all over the walls."

"Don't worry, I'll paint them," I promised.

"I know you will, but you're scaring me. You disappeared. You didn't answer your phone. Nobody knew where you were. Now you magically reappear one night when I'm not home and almost overdose? Look at this place. Have you gone mad? How do I even read this?" she said, pointing to the nearest quote and reading skeptically, *"I want to keep thinking about great and brave American nights. People who go out and make things happen, no matter what the cost."*

There was silence. I stared blankly until she continued.

"Myles, who are you talking about? Is this for the book?"

I'd meant the quote as a mocking comment about the cheapness of American patriotism. Spoken by Ari's character, and glossed with a little narrative context, the lines might have resonated, but Nathalie was a poor actress. She read everything monotone.

"That's only a fragment, Nat," I said. "They're all fragments. I ran out of paper. That's what happened. I needed more space. I'll paint the walls. You don't have to worry."

"But I *am* worried," she insisted.

I suggested we watch something to clear our heads. We streamlined a news program on Nathalie's computer, but neither one of us was paying any attention. Nathalie was fretting over dozens of conversations that she wanted to start with me. I was still trying to piece together my disjointed memories and writing. I'd been to Joel's. I remembered that much. I'd spent days avoiding Alan and Dylan. Then I discovered a handful of crumpled receipts in my pocket. One was from a pizza joint in Times Square, several others were from Midtown and Lower East Side bars. Evidently, I'd spent three nights at a hostel up in Harlem.

Nat saw me fidgeting with the papers. "I hope you didn't spend too much," she said.

I checked my wallet. At least I hadn't lost my credit card. Nat wasn't impressed. She stood up. "Myles, rent? Please tell me you can pay," she asked.

That was the end of her sympathy. When she saw me smile, she slammed the computer shut and stormed out of the apartment. Minutes later, she was back, carrying a stack of mail from our box downstairs.

"Do you ever check the mail? Myles, there are two months' worth of bills here."

Nathalie dumped the letters over my head. "You didn't pay these!" she yelled, holding up the electric and phone bills. "You promised." When she opened my credit card statement, there was a moment of shocked silence, then an explosion.

"Five thousand dollars! Are you insane? What the hell were you thinking?"

Nat threw on her coat and kicked my manuscript on her way out. I chased after her.

"I want you out!" she screamed as we scrambled down the staircase. "You're a waste, Myles. You're a fucking waste of life."

I caught up to her at the door and barred her from leaving.

"Let me go!" she said, squirming. Her voice was as shrill as a rape whistle.

I covered her mouth with my hand until tears swelled in her eyes. Then I stepped back.

"Nat?"

She touched my lip, and that abrasion on my cheek. I knew I was feverish.

"I mean it," she said. "This isn't working. We have to stop."

I shrugged my shoulders, admitting defeat. "I'm sorry."

"I know. I'm sorry, too."

"I'll send you the book?"

"I'd like that."

"I need some time to finish."

"Time is good."

"I love you."

Nat kissed me. She kissed me slow, sorry and salty from all the tears. Then the door clicked open, and she wandered outside. I followed her, but it was a mere formality. She hailed a cab. I barely received a parting glance before she sped away into the bright, busy morning.

12:10 A.M.,
Thursday, March 6, 2008

I kept running, splashing through my reflection in the puddles. Soon, Jeremy's music, that scratchy voice Ari introduced me to when he sent his brother's CD, filled my ears. Like a good song on the radio, it became my mood—nostalgic. I remembered tinkering with my guitar one night in Nathalie's bedroom while searching for the band's imaginary sound. That was before our break-up. Nat sat at her sewing machine, working on a flapper costume for a show. The steady rhythm of the needle provided a metronome for my experiment. Adding country riffs and capoing up the scale, I stood behind her, singing silly songs in my mock, Johnny Cash voice, making her laugh.

I started running again. If I walked, my thinking went in circles. When I ran, I distracted myself with the book's characters—Ari, Beth and Jeremy. Their voices offered a convenient escape. I put my mind inside Ari's and witnessed the novel's climactic scene of destruction take place in a lonely cowboy bar out in desolate Wyoming. The band I had created was quarreling during a performance. There was a raging forest fire in the background, and everyone was tired as hell.

Ari's soliloquy began with frustration, guilt and apathy. I saw the towers crashing, bloody newsreels from the wars, the President talking about his faith, everything symbolized America's confused patriotism.

"All I'm saying is, I thought I could understand," I heard Ari's character say, dry and passive. Stopping in a dark alley, I moved my lips around the words, trying to feel out every aspect of the voice. Then I was shivering uncontrollably, terrified of stepping back into the nightmare streets where everyone was real.

I tried to be practical, but as long as I was in that alley I couldn't move. I wanted to bang my head against a wall, anything to break the spell and quiet my mad thinking. Where was Ari? Was he still in Times Square? Had he gone downtown? Where would he hide? Did Ari know what had happened to Chris and Ethan? Would he seek out Hailey? And What about Alan? Would he turn himself in to save Ethan? Would he confess and implicate me? I had never fought anyone so savagely.

I needed money. I had only two dollars left in my pocket. Lee's "lucky" bill wasn't even enough for a subway ride downtown. How could we have let Jim and Sam escape with all that cash? Sam shot Ethan. Sam shot Ethan. Sam shot Ethan. Terrible refrains rang in my head.

I picked up the pace again and didn't stop until I'd reached the East River. I crossed the FDR highway to the Esplanade and walked North along the water, up to Carl Schurz Park. I knew it was a long shot, but I thought I might find Ari there. He and Hailey had exchanged their first kisses on a bench overlooking the river. They'd often go back there to make up whenever they'd had a fight.

Nice try. The park bench was empty. I sat down and tapped my fingers on the rusty armrest, watching the murky river run past. Miriam and I had kissed here, too.

Miriam
(October 2007)

Out of the blue, I received a text from Miriam. She wanted to meet. I barely remembered her. Was she that older woman I flirted with at the Sony Club? I typed a hasty, 'yes,' and left the apartment.

We met at a midtown bar, got a little drunk and drew on postcards with oil pastels I'd stolen from Chris.

"I haven't drawn like this since I was in high school," Miriam laughed, showing me her comic frog doodle. She knew I was looking down her shirt. There was a bit of black lace peeking up out of the shadows of her curves, and I was lost.

"Another round?" I offered, shrugging off embarrassment.

Miriam agreed, but she was determined to keep me on my toes. "You definitely don't know how to write women," she criticized my writing while we waited for the bartender to draw the shamrock in the Guinness he had poured for me. "Beth is a ridiculous fantasy."

I was surprised. I didn't even remember giving her my manuscript. Miriam saw my face and helped me understand.

"You don't remember, do you? I don't blame you. You were doused when you dropped your book off. You left the manuscript at my office three weeks ago. My secretary said you reeked. She almost called security."

"Why didn't she?"

"You had good references," Miriam laughed, showing me that stained napkin on which she'd written her contact information. I'd paper-clipped it to my manuscript. "I started picking," she continued. "Now I'm reading it again."

"But you don't like the lead female character?"

"How can I? Beth? That's her name, right?"

I nodded.

"Beth is totally idealized. You make her too innocent, too sad and too beautiful. A real woman would be conscious of her faults and try to compensate. She'd be difficult. A bitch."

"Do you like the other characters?"

"Jeremy is very funny. Ari is serious. I like their dynamic. I'm wondering which of them is you."

"And the plot?"

"The plot is sound. Everything is good except for the girl."

I wasn't satisfied with that answer. Beth was a central character. If she came off badly, then the whole novel was rotten.

"If you don't like the characters, why read the book again?"

Miriam finished her drink and licked her lips with a pointy tongue.

"I'm very bored, Myles," she said. The phrase sounded wonderfully rehearsed. Her hand was on top of mine. She felt the writers' callous on my finger. When she noticed a spot of green pastel on her fingernail, however, she retreated.

"Water, please?" she asked the bartender. He brought her a glass and she immediately dipped her finger into the water, rubbing out the stain. Then she searched her purse for a credit card.

"You have to go?" I asked.

"I do."

"Let me pay?"

"No."

"When will I see you again?"

"Tonight. If you want."

"Dinner?"

"No. Not dinner. I eat too early for you. Will you come uptown? It's Friday. The Whitney Museum is open late."

Damn erotic shadows. Miriam was full of them, practically flickering depths and secrets. I thought about her all day.

"Aren't you cold?" Miriam asked me when I arrived at the museum later that night without a jacket. She had changed out of her business dress into tight blue jeans and a cozy brown sweater. A white, fluffy scarf circled her neck. She kept it on when we checked her pea coat at the entrance. Then we waltzed around the museum together, admiring the Calder mobiles and splatter-Pollocks.

"You know what Vonnegut says when he's at a museum?" I asked, pointing to a wall of paintings.

"Isn't he dead?" Miriam reminded me.

"Said," I corrected myself. "Vonnegut *said* you have to go through the museum fast. Like this:" I jogged ahead of her and doubled back. "The sensation is best on roller skates. Then all you have to do is think, 'this one, yes! That one, no,' and presto, suddenly you realize the meaning of life."

I thought Miriam would smile. She didn't.

"But Vonnegut's dead," Miriam said again, turning away to look at a large Picasso. I was surprised. I loved the challenge of making her laugh.

We walked out of the museum into a cold, crisp night. I made a stupid bet that we could see the moon from the Esplanade. The moon was supposed to be full and oddly colored that night. When we reached the river, however, light pollution already filled the sky with fluorescent haze.

"I remember the night sky out west," I told her. "The Milky Way looks as thick as smoke."

She knew the scene I was referring to in my book.

"To tell you the truth, Myles, I liked that part in your novel—When the band is stuck in New Mexico. Beth is tolerable then, and I liked the mood. I liked the colors too. Have you been there?"

"I was. Ari and me. We went out there together a few years ago. Our friend, Dylan, joined us on the way back. We were out there when the U.S. started bombing Iraq."

Miriam put her head on my shoulder. For whatever reason, she wanted me to keep talking about my friends. The conversation was pleasant until I asked her where she'd been when the war news hit.

She said she didn't remember.

"Come on. I don't believe you. I'll never forget those war speeches. We listened to NPR on the radio non-stop, the whole drive west from San Antonio. Ari and I couldn't get enough of that. We thought it was ridiculous. People were counting down the seconds. Tell me where you were."

"No," Miriam said, slightly annoyed. She lifted her head briefly, then put her chin back on my shoulder.

"Why not?" I persisted. Miriam sat up and looked out across the river.

"Please don't," she insisted. We stared each other down. Finally, I let my question drop. Silence reigned. In the dark, I realized I could kiss her.

Back at Miriam's brownstone, we kissed wildly, undressed, and dove under the bed covers. Suddenly Miriam stopped me.

"I want you to tell me about *her*," she said.

"Come on. You don't want to know any of that."

She started to get out of bed. I asked *who,* in particular, interested her.

"Don't give me that crap," she pressed. "You know perfectly well." Then she softened. Cautiously returning to bed, Miriam let me kiss her again. For a moment, I thought all our tension was gone, but she soon stiffened and rolled over. "Your muse," she muttered, her back to me. "Tell me about the girl behind Beth."

Everything slowed down. I put my head on top of hers and hugged her side. We were both wet between the legs, my sap cold and sticky, hers, warm and dribbling. She lifted a finger and pointed to my manuscript on her nightstand. I clutched her heavy breast and explored her swollen nipple. She coldly removed my hand.

We waited each other out. Testing: trading skin for secrets, penetration for truths. When it became clear that I wouldn't say anything revealing about Nathalie or Beth, eventually Miriam relented.

"Just don't treat me fragile," she warned, making me look in her eyes. Her expression was brutally pessimistic.

12:15 A.M.,
Thursday, March 6, 2008

The shivers stopped. My heartbeat slowed. My fingers went white with cold. When I noticed new spots of blood on my clothes, I thought of climbing down off the pier to wash the stains out in the river water. Then I remembered Murphy's Irish proverb: "The river be but a stone's throw away from debts," he'd always say when he handed out our weekly pay. "But even the weariest rivers wind somehow safe to sea." Of course, Murphy was mocking us with that rhyme. He knew the debts that we were taking on would drown us all.

I stood up and started toward Miriam's. She was the only one who could help me now. Her place was way up in Harlem. I never understood why she insisted on living there. Miriam owned several houses around the country, yet her family's old brownstone was somehow sacred, and she didn't mind the long ride downtown to her office.

Miriam's house was spooky, overdone with ornate furniture, antique mirrors and brassy light fixtures. When I stayed there, I liked to look at the portrait of her grandfather that hung above the winding stairs. His wrinkled face and disheveled clothes made me imagine the trials faced by her immigrant family. He'd escaped the pogroms in Russia to pedal fruit and bread in New York. Miriam said this man was so illiterate that he couldn't even spell the name of his village, or find it on a map. All that mattered was that his children had food and weren't persecuted. He married a Hungarian woman. Their son—Miriam's father—was the first in the family to go to college. Her father was also the one who bought their house. Now most of her family had passed. She rarely spoke about her husband, but I knew he had disappointed her somehow. There were no children, and he'd gone missing. On Friday nights, she'd light candles and say the Mourner's Kaddish.

How could I refuse when Miriam invited me to celebrate Hanukkah with her in Florida? The trip was glamorous. We toured the Sunshine State in a black convertible, taking in the big blue sky, the steaming Everglades, and the purple puff clouds that hover over the ocean in the evening sky. Miriam didn't like eating out. She cooked Hungarian-Jewish—blintzes, strudels, stuffed cabbage—and in the evenings, we took long walks before we lit the festival candles.

There was a pool behind the condo. Miriam enjoyed watching me swim in the mornings. She'd fix Bloody Marys and sunbathe with her top off. When I joined her under the palm trees and Spanish moss, she'd always have a towel ready and a prying business question on her mind.

"What do you make of this stock?" she'd ask, showing me some symbol or chart in the Wall Street Journal. "Your friends are buying," she'd say, strutting away from me. Obviously she knew about Jim and Sam's inside trades.

If I didn't have an answer, she'd call me useless and swat me with the paper. Once she grilled me about Murphy:

"Don't you know he's being investigated?"

I didn't.

"His papers aren't in order. He shouldn't be in the country."

"I thought he has a visa?"

"The document must be a forgery. He's laundering money, Myles. That man is a crook. My husband…"

She'd stop herself and close up. Somehow her disappeared husband and Murphy were connected, but I could never get her to tell. Maybe it didn't matter. To some extent, Miriam was no different from Nathalie. She couldn't help wanting to test my patience, and the manipulative lies she told were usually so thinly veiled that I considered them her way of telling the truth. Besides, our emotions were so raw during those first months that most of what we could tell each other was pointless conversation. The sex was supposed to be convenient, the talk witty.

I'd play romantic when it pleased her mood. On New Year's Eve, I used Ari's line, saying, "what do you say we try falling in love this winter?"

Miriam rolled her eyes. "Save the mushy stuff for your book," she replied.

She'd been a good friend to me all year, although we stopped sleeping together after the holidays. Instead, she'd drag me to book talks, readings and other publishing events. She loved taking me to the movies. Coincidence? Before everyone left for the square that night, Miriam had called. I didn't answer, and she didn't leave a message, but that was all understandable. We hadn't seen each other in over a month.

Outside her brownstone, I rang the doorbell. No reply. I knew she was there. Her light was on. She wanted to make me sweat. At the corner of the street, there was an all-night fruit vendor. I bought two golden apples—Miriam's favorite—with Lee's two-dollar bill. Then I returned to her doorstep and rang again. This time I looked straight into the video camera she used for security, brandishing the apples as though I were making an offering to a goddess. My ploy worked. She buzzed me in and stood at her door, ready to hold me.

"You're hurt?" she asked, immediately noticing the blood stains on my shirt.

I shook my head.

"Is it Ari?"

I nodded. She knew everything else simply by holding me.

We hugged for as long as she could tolerate. Then she took the apples and pulled away.

"You stink," she said. "Take a shower. I made goulash. I'll warm some up."

Reunion
(November 2007)

Then Miriam led Ari to me. Over a month had passed since Nathalie asked me to move out. I hadn't seen her once. What the hell. I felt guilty, but I figured I'd move my things into her room. I was sick of sleeping on my leaky air mattress. With nobody around nagging me, there was little motivating me to pack up and find a new place. Besides, I finally had my own apartment in New York City. I wasn't about to give that up easily.

At first, I was mad at Nathalie. Everything I did in that apartment was out of spite. I brought a girl home from the bar, and we fucked on Nathalie's bed. I started my own mural with Chris' crayons. I refused to clean. After a week, the place was falling apart, and I felt ashamed. I was out of control, and I missed seeing Nathalie dance around in costume while she practiced her lines. Growing depressed, I decided a weekend getaway was the only way to clear my head. Then I called my Grandpa.

The phone rang and rang. I was awful worried until he picked up.

"Hello?" I finally heard Sol yell into the phone, compensating for his failing hearing.

"Grandpa, it's me, Myles," I had to explain twice. Then we made plans.

"Sure, come visit," Sol said, relaxing. "We'll have Shabbat."

That phone call made me laugh. I loved my Grandfather. Sol had always been a great inspiration to me, and I missed him dearly. Lately, however, I felt as though I needed to put on a mask before I could visit. I couldn't stand the way his body was deteriorating. He'd been in and out of the hospital all year. I knew he was dying, but I wasn't willing to accept that he was sick.

Sol was the war hero in my family. The stoic example of honorable manhood I'd followed throughout my youth, and strayed from in my adolescence. He had held a foxhole against a German ambush at the Battle of the Bulge, and he kept his collection of war trophies—German Lugers, Kraut helmets, a jar of sand from Normandy—on a shelf in his study. He was eighty-nine now. He knew five languages, was writing his memoirs and could still play Yiddish tunes on his fiddle, whenever I brought my guitar along. I simply couldn't imagine him passing.

Luckily, I caught Sol on a good day, and he sounded excited to see me. I was happy too. I knew my mom would be pleased to find out I'd made the trip. She'd been begging me to visit for months already, serving up a heavy dose of guilt whenever she called.

"He's only an hour away. How can you be so selfish?" was her crying refrain. "Sol's dying, Myles. You won't have many more chances to see your grandfather."

No sweat. Now I wanted to go. I bought a ticket for the four o'clock train to Middletown, arriving shortly before sundown and printed it out. That gave me the morning and afternoon to write and dig the city. After that, I was feeling cocky. I knew I'd done something good, and I'd convinced myself that if I made a conscious effort to show good intentions every-

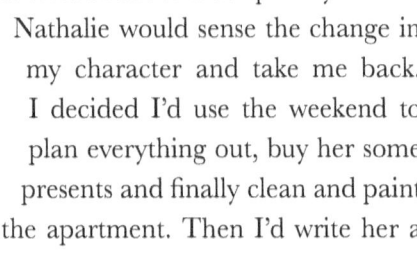

where I went, then the mitzvahs and karma would start to add up. Maybe even Nathalie would sense the change in my character and take me back. I decided I'd use the weekend to plan everything out, buy her some presents and finally clean and paint the apartment. Then I'd write her a good, old-fashioned letter.

I pinned my train ticket to Nathalie's big, antique mirror and combed my hair hipster. Strange, I hardly recognized my reflection. I'd lost weight. I looked pale. When I discovered that old, gray suit Jim had lent me, lying crinkled in the closet, the costume was a pass to an inspired adventure. I couldn't resist the plot. Time to buy that hat, I told myself as I grabbed my guitar and headed for the door. To get Nathalie back, I'd need some props.

At the hat store on 38th and Eighth Avenue, I chose a brushed, brown leather fedora and passed my credit card through their machine. Rejected. No problem. I had one of Professor Murphy's hundred-dollar bills stuffed in my pocket, and I knew Grandpa would be good for a bailout check later.

I felt as though I was getting the best of everyone. From surfing job sites at the library a day earlier, I knew of a free lunch for writers taking place at the Marriott Marquis. Some failing company wanted public feedback regarding their website. Again, no problem. I was starved and full of free advice. I spent the lunch hour in a conference room on the 30th floor of that skyscraper, dealing Subway cold cuts, peering down at bright Times Square, boldly suggesting, "Pass the salt, pass the pepper," and barely paying attention to the company's presentation.

Afterward, I became curious about the publishing conference going on downstairs. The big banner read, "The Future of Books!" As I rode the escalator down to the lobby, I spotted Miriam working a booth in the corner of the conference hall. I rushed to meet her.

"So this is the Kindle?" I asked, sitting down among all the attendees who wanted to hear her pitch. Cautiously, she smiled.

"I like your hat," Miriam said.

"I don't see any of *my* books on here," I complained, turning the display eBook apparatus upside down and on its side.

"Don't be vain. It's not a toy," Miriam scolded, taking the tablet away from me.

"I'm sorry."

"You're not sorry."

"I'm a little bit sorry."

"Where are you going?" she said, curious about the guitar. I showed her my train ticket.

"What time do you leave?"

"Five."

"Do you have time for a drink?"

"I do."

"Get us a table at O'Lunncy's on 45th and Sixth. I'll be there in twenty."

No kisses in public, not even on the cheek.

Forty minutes later, Miriam stormed into the pub. I was sitting at the bar. She slid in next to me and ordered a whiskey.

"Where did you learn to drink like that?" I asked when she gulped hers down, wiped her lips and ordered another.

"Shut up, Myles. There's something I need to ask you."

"Shoot," I said, straightening up for an interrogation.

"That night we met. At the Sony Club. What were you doing there? Tell me the truth."

"Beats me. A couple of stooges dragged me."

"What were their names?"

"Jim Cohen, and Sam Burkowitz."

"I knew it."

"Knew what?"

"That night, after the concert, you went downstairs with the pianist. How do you know Bernard Murphy?"

"I used to work for him."

"Where?"

"He runs a salon for veterans. I worked on their anti-war publication."

"Tell me you quit, Myles. Please tell me you don't work for that man anymore."

"No," I said, shaking my head. "I left that work."

"Good," Miriam said. "Do you know Murphy well?"

"Well enough to know he's not what he seems."

Miriam didn't like me being cagey. She stared me down.

"Myles, I don't want you to chase this Ari you've been writing about anymore. He's mixed up in something bad."

"How do you know anything about Ari besides what's in my book? Everything I write is at least fifty percent fiction, Miriam. Don't forget that."

"Never mind. Just promise me you won't see him anymore."

"I'll visit Ari whenever I want. Come on, cut this out. Why are you so worried?"

"When a stranger comes up to me and says he knows I'm sleeping with a kid, and that he has to speak to you on behalf of Bernard Murphy, I get a little freaked out, Myles. Nobody should know about my personal life. Especially one of *your* friends."

"You saw Ari? Are you sure it was him?"

"Unless he was lying about his name, I'm sure. He fit your description perfectly."

"Just now?"

"Back at the hotel."

I was startled. Had I been so difficult to find that Murphy felt he needed to send all his agents after me? The funny thing was, if Ari had called me directly, I would have gladly picked up. It was the others I wanted to dodge.

"I guess he's finally back from Ireland. I have to warn him about Murphy," I said, starting to get anxious. "Do you think he saw me? Did he follow you? Is he still there?"

Miriam drained her glass dry, watching me garble every sentence. "Why can't you move on already?" She asked. "Myles, I know your whole story. I know what you're trying to do with this apology you've written. Haven't you taken your belief in comradeship a bit too far?"

She didn't let me answer. Instead, Miriam began to rant:

"Murphy's a creep," she insisted. "I don't know everything, but I know his business isn't honest. My colleagues at Lehman Brother's have dealt with Murphy and Jim Cohen before. I wouldn't trust anyone on his payroll."

"Maybe. But come on, Miriam, that's not fair. By telling me to stay away you're hardly being proactive. You're better than that. Why are you protecting Murphy? If he's such a dirty player then why don't you or one of your business cronies call his bluff?"

"It's more complicated than that. A lot of money is involved. People could go to jail."

"How unfair."

"Cut the socialist rhetoric, Mr. Ivy League. You certainly have no trouble taking Murphy's money *and* mine."

"Sure I took the money. Murphy paid me well enough. But I did get out, didn't I? Besides, I never cared about the work. I was there for Ari. Now you're telling me that my friend is in over his head? I'm sure as hell not going to wait around and let him make a mistake."

"Let it go, Myles, please? For me? I want to help you. I do. I want to publish your book, and I want you to have a proud career. I promise you, if you get involved with Murphy and his boys again, nothing good will come."

I couldn't listen to her. Miriam didn't know or value any of the things Ari and I had been through together. She couldn't understand what it meant to me to keep my friend from getting hurt. I had to warn Ari about Murphy's violent streak. "Is he still at the hotel?" I asked again.

"He's waiting for you," she muttered, unable to look at me.

I knew I'd hurt her feelings. She wanted me to need her, and her matronly instincts were saying, "protect him."

I gathered up my things, stood up to finish my beer, and told her I'd call on Sunday when I got back into the city.

"Don't bother," she warned.

"Come on. You wanted to go to that reading, remember?"

Earlier that week Miriam had invited me to an open mic session at a downtown café. She wanted me to read one of the chapters from my book. Now she changed her mind.

"Will you read something different?"

"I can."

"Good. If you're set on seeing your friend, fine. I respect that. But I won't listen to you talk about him anymore. You got that? I won't read a word you write about him either. I'm not interested in watching you fuck up your life."

I tipped my hat and kissed her cheek.

"Goodbye, Miriam. Thank you."

She pulled me close, kissing me hard before letting go.

12:30 A.M.,
Thursday, March 6, 2008

Miriam left a pile of folded clean clothes on the bathroom counter for me to change into after I showered. I guess they'd belonged to her husband. When I came out, she circled me, testing the fit of the pants and adjusting the collar on the striped shirt she'd lent me. It was no use. Her husband was a bigger man than me. I looked shabby in his dress, and Miriam was disappointed.

"Where are my things?" I asked. Miriam pointed to the fireplace where she had lit a warm blaze. My clothes were lying in a pile on the stone mantle. I followed her across the room.

"Don't tell me whose blood this is," she said, emptying the pockets of my soiled pants before stuffing them into the fire. The clothes steamed, then burst into flames.

"No names either," Miriam added, making the rules of her house clear. "I'll help you tonight, but I don't want to know any details."

I hung my head. When I started to yawn, Miriam ushered me to the kitchen table and told me to sit down. Then she placed a steaming bowl of warm, red goulash, clumped with potatoes, carrots and strands of soft, soup-soaked beef in front of me. Her cooking looked and smelled delicious, but my appetite was fleeting. Under different circumstances, I would have devoured the portion and asked for seconds. Worried, Miriam sat down across from me.

"You need money, don't you?" she asked.

I nodded.

"After you eat."

I nodded again and forced myself to take a bite.

"Tell me the last place you saw him?" she asked about Ari.

"In the apartment. This evening. Around five."

"What was his mood? Could you tell anything?"

"He was quiet. He kept cleaning his gun and checking his face in the mirror. He made a little speech before they left."

"What's their plan?"

"I thought you didn't want to know?"

"Do I?"

I shrugged my shoulders and asked to borrow her computer.

Miriam went to the desk in her bedroom and brought out her laptop. This time she sat down next to me. We looked up the news and that Times Square live feed. There was still nothing violent being reported. No sign of my friends either. I explained their plot, how everyone had cowered, and that now I needed to find Ari before Murphy killed anyone else.

"Where would he go, Myles? You must have some idea."

I thought for a while, finally concluding that I needed Hailey's help.

"Hailey?"

"Ari's girlfriend. She was at the apartment earlier looking for him. I blew her off."

Miriam looked at me bewildered. "I don't see how I can help," she said.

"Let me use your phone?" I asked. "Hailey is mad at me. She won't pick up when I call. If she doesn't recognize the number, she'll think Ari is calling."

Miriam liked the idea. She brought me her landline phone and put it on speaker. I dialed.

Hailey picked up immediately. "Ari? Hello? Who's calling?"

"It's me, Myles."

"Fuck you."

"I'm sorry."

"Unless you know where Ari is, I don't want to talk."

"Please, I can explain."

"I know you were at that apartment earlier. I can't believe you'd do that to me."

She hung up. I let a minute go by before I tried again. This time Hailey let it ring until her voicemail clicked on. A minute later she called me back.

"Alright, spill it," she demanded.

"Ari's gone to Times Square. We have to find him."

"Is he in trouble?"

"I don't know. Where can I meet you?"

"I don't trust you or any of his friends. Tell me right now if my fiancé is in trouble. Then I'll decide if we meet tonight."

"Fiancé?"

"We were keeping it a secret. He proposed last week."

"I had no idea."

"Myles, why is Ari doing this? He won't return my calls. I don't know where he is. He's been acting strange all week. What's happened? Tell me!"

"There's no time. Listen; I'm three blocks from the sub-way. I'll be in Times Square in thirty minutes. Meet me there."

This time I hung up. I hated fighting over the phone and I figured Hailey's curiosity would get the best of her. She'd meet me. I wasn't worried.

I stood up too fast and was dizzy.

"You'll be cold without a jacket," Miriam fussed. She pointed to the closet and told me to pick out something I liked. Meanwhile, she found her purse and counted out several twenty-dollar bills.

"Will that be enough?" she asked, finishing her drink.

"Thank you," I said, reaching for the cash.

Miriam didn't let go. "Don't come back here if you kill somebody," she said.

"I'll call you when I find Ari," I promised.

"No, Myles. Don't bother. It's obvious how this ends."

"So this is goodbye?"

"Unless you forget something."

I needed a minute to understand. The Luger. I was about to leave without my weapon.

Returning Stranger

(November 2007)

I didn't realize how angry I was at Ari for abandoning me to face Murphy alone, until I saw him standing outside the Marriott Marquis.

"Leaving town?" he asked.

I walked right past him.

"Come on, Myles, what's this about?" he called after me.

I picked up the pace, dodging the Times Square costume crowd and sprinting down 8th Avenue toward Penn Station. Ari kept on my heels.

We arrived in the nick of time. Inside the station, the gate was open for my train, and they were already issuing the last call for passengers. Ari followed me down the escalator to the platform. I boarded, and he leapt in after me.

"Are you mad? You better have cash on you," I said, pushing him away from me while I caught my breath and rearranged my bags.

"Where are you going, Myles? You're not skipping town again, are you?"

"Give me one good reason why I should tell you?"

Unfortunately, I didn't get a chance to withhold this information. The conductor appeared behind us, asking for our tickets.

"Middletown. That's fourteen dollars," the big black man said, punching holes in my receipt as Ari dug out his wallet.

I didn't wait around for Ari to finish paying. I took off down the aisle and dove into the first open seat I found, hoping I could hide from him.

A minute later, I felt Ari's eyes on me. I wouldn't look.

He sat down across from me. "I take it we're going to your Grandpa's house?" he said, grinning.

I stared out the window, but there was nothing to see. We were still in the dark of the tunnel underneath the Hudson River.

"I remember your Grandpa Sol," Ari continued. He was thinking of the trip to Florida we took together in college. We spent a week at my Grandfather's condo. Ari loved the old man. He loved Sol's New York accent and his Yiddish mannerisms. He loved the courageous war stories, his speeches on Israel and the music we'd play together.

"Is he very sick?"

"Cancer. He stopped the chemo. He feels better now, but he doesn't have long."

"I'm sorry, Myles, I know you were close."

"We *are* close," I corrected.

"Right... Suppose you base a character on your grandfather?" Ari suggested. I knew he was trying to manipulate the conversation, but I was surprised that he'd go to my soft spot and bring up the book. Suddenly, he was full of creative ideas. "Someone has to represent patience and wisdom in the novel," he elaborated. "Otherwise there's no balance. Maybe an older man plays in the band? I think every instrument should be symbolic of a certain personality—"

"Ari, what the fuck? Where have you been?" I said, cutting him off.

"A lot of people are asking the same thing about you."

The train sped out of the tunnel. Finally, I got a good look at my friend. He was dressed up in a suit for the book conference, but he didn't look well. I could tell he was exhausted. His skin was bad, his hair was long, and he was constantly forcing smiles.

"I'm through with Murphy," I said.

"I'm sorry to hear that."

"I think you should quit that group too, Ari. Nothing is right about that man."

"You mean because Murphy roughed you up a little?"

I nodded, showing him as much sarcasm as I could muster. "He more than roughed me up," I said. "I had bruises."

"You're over-reacting," Ari argued. "Think of it as a rite of passage. There's a lot at stake here. Murphy wasn't sure if he could trust you, so he pressed you for some information."

"Rite of passage? What are you saying? What information?"

"You knew I was in Ireland, but you didn't tell."

"You mean it was a test?" I said, stunned.

"A test you passed well. Come back to our group, Myles. Murphy meant you no harm, and now he'll pay you double. Everybody goes through a little initiation. "

"Initiation? What the hell, Ari. Don't you think this is going too far? This isn't a fraternity. Tell me you didn't know he was going to treat me like that."

"Of course I knew. We decided together that you needed to be vetted."

"Is that why you went away?"

"No, I went to see my brother.
That was completely unrelated. You
know that."

"I can't believe you set me up for

187

a beating. First Ethan almost throws me off the fire escape at that apartment party. Then Jim and Sam practically drug me into a coma with pills. Next thing I know, your professor is kicking me in the gut. I don't care who gave the orders, these people are psycho."

"Don't be so dramatic. You're imagining things. Only Murphy knew where I'd gone on vacation. Ethan was drunk and belligerent. Jim and Sam simply wanted to show you a good time. And from what I hear, you *did* have plenty of fun that night. Afterwards too. I spoke to Joel. He said he hasn't seen you sober in weeks. Looks like you made a new girlfriend on your binge as well."

"Why are you guys following me? It's creepy."

"Myles, you disappeared. We had to check up on you. You understand, don't you? You know sensitive information. Besides, you're on Murphy's payroll. He has a right to ask after an employee who doesn't show up to work."

"You were gone over a month. Murphy didn't seem to have any pressing questions. Instead, he took everything out on me."

"That was different. We all went through the same initiation. Like I said, consider it a rite of passage. I was supposed to take care of yours, but then I was away."

"I think I would have preferred having you initiate me."

"You wouldn't take me seriously. It's better that Murphy interrogated you. You showed courage and he respects you now. Besides, I don't think I could hit you."

"Why not? Are you afraid you'd get carried away? Because of Melissa?"

"Are you serious? Damn it, Myles, I told you I'm over that. You're mixing everything up. When are you going to understand that showing a little blood for this cause isn't bad? All

Murphy wanted was to see how your mind works under pressure, how tightly your lips are sealed and if you're loyal. Now he can trust you."

"Right, 'show a little blood.' That's what Murphy is grooming us for."

"Commitment," Ari corrected. "Show commitment. I think that's a better phrase."

"Call it whatever you want. You're not going to make me forget what Murphy said to me. He was raving mad, kicking me and calling me an informer. He said that's why he pays me. The man is power crazy. That's obvious."

"Shh, Myles, you're yelling."

We both paused to look around. We'd turned heads across the aisle with our heated talk, but the startled passengers all looked away when we stared them down.

"This is ridiculous," I continued in a throaty whisper. "I'm not going to hide what I think. I can't believe you're so devoted to Murphy. He's manipulating you."

"He's not manip—"

"He's certainly filling all your friends' heads up with a lot of hot, empty rhetoric. Don't you see? He knows boys like Ethan and Landon are impressionable. They'll always need someone ordering them around. It was the same when they joined the army. They followed Old Glory and promised to *'free Iraq.'* All Murphy has to do is pose as Uncle Sam and make his boys feel proud. They'll do anything he wants. He's made them his pawns. You too, maybe."

"That was eloquent, Myles, but I don't buy it. Especially coming from you. We were on the road together when Bush was shocking and awing Baghdad, don't forget. You talked like a radical. You were angry as hell. That's why I recommended you to Murphy. I thought you'd be on our side. Here's the man who will actually act to counter the injustices you used to rail about, and you can't bring yourself to trust him? I don't believe you. Murphy's rhetoric isn't empty. Deep down, I know you sympathize with what we're advocating."

"That doesn't erase the fact that your leader attacked me. Who cares how my opinion of the war fits into your movement? I don't need my principles dragged out of me. Especially when I'm lying on the ground, defenseless. There are better ways to figure a man out," I said, furious that Ari refused to admit I'd been abused.

"Maybe. But to tell you the truth, you did well. I heard you even talked back a little."

"I can't listen to this," I said, turning away and staring out the window. Outside, the sun was setting. We were past the rusty, industrial sprawl, entering the Jersey woods and suburbs. The fall was waning. October's crisp and brightly colored leaves had all fallen away, fluttering in the cold winds and rain. Now they shriveled and crumbled in thick piles of mulch that covered lawns and sidewalks. I was thinking: I'd like to get away from everyone in the city, get relaxed and go for a walk in the forest by myself. Ari interrupted my reverie.

"You're always looking to escape, aren't you, Myles?" he criticized. "Stay too long in the city and you only wind up digging holes for yourself. Am I right?"

I shook my head in weak defense. Ari always made me feel so cowardly.

"Look, Myles, we're willing to let you take some time off, if that's what you need. Why don't you spend the weekend in the country? You can even go up to Ithaca for a bit if you like. Murphy will pay you over your vacation, but when you get back, we need your help."

I watched the woods and the pastures, the cows and the little Jersey cottages passing by. I had been rotting in the city so long I'd forgotten how liberating a grid-less landscape feels. But Ari was on to me. He seemed to know my thoughts.

"You've been cooped up too long, Myles," He said. "How long has it been since you've gone out of town?"

"I lost count after Nathalie left. Almost six months?"

"She's gone?"

"I was binging. I wrote all over the walls in our apartment. She's not coming back."

"That explains the older woman?"

"Miriam? No, that's something new. I like her. She invited me to Florida for the holidays. She wants to publish my book. Tell me again how you know about us?"

Ari started to tell me how Jim and Sam had helped him pick up the trail, but his excuses for spying were becoming redundant. He had an easy justification for every intrusion he'd made into my life and didn't seem to realize how his actions undermined our friendship.

"Never mind," I interrupted, desperate to change the subject. "I don't want to talk about this anymore. I need time to think. That's all. Ok?"

"Take your time," Ari said. "I understand."

Ten minutes went by without us saying anything to each other. Finally, I asked him about his trip to Ireland and thanked him again for the concert tickets he had sent me.

"Feels like forever ago."

"When did you get back?"

"Almost a month. By the way, Hailey was asking about you while we were abroad. She said you never called back about visiting her class."

"Shoot. I forgot."

"She was excited to have you play music for her kids."

"Is it too late?"

"No. But she doesn't expect you to come anymore."

"I'll call tomorrow. I promise."

Ari shook his head and rubbed under his glasses. When he looked up again, I saw how beleaguered, even a little sad, he looked.

"Ari, what's going on? Didn't you have fun with Jeremy?" I asked.

"We did, and we didn't. My brother is going to stay in Ireland. He's got nothing. No visa, nothing. But he can't stand life in the States. I thought he'd come back with me and that we could live close by for a while. Maybe even work together."

"For Murphy?"

"Why not? He'd pay him well."

"You mean buy him."

"Come on, you don't really think that about Murphy, do you?"

"Jesus, are you blind? Ari, he's bought everybody."

"Here we go again. Look, Myles, I know right now you don't think much of Murphy, but if you'd been with us in the beginning, when Chris, Landon and Ethan first got back from the war, you'd see things differently. Murphy saved their lives. He got them off the PTS drugs. He coached them out of suicidal depressions. He gave them something to work toward and live for. Professor Murphy is a great man. You might not approve of his methods. You might question his motives, but what he's proposing; the way he's inspiring us—even when this war has gotten so out of hand and the economy keeps spiraling—I think it's beautiful. If we want to do something to influence the election, professor Murphy is our only hope."

"You've got your leader. I don't see why you need me."

"We need everyone," Ari corrected me. "You don't realize your value. The way you write the soldier's stories and help get the men talking…. You ask the right questions, and you're exactly the kind of reporter we need spreading our message."

"And what message is that?"

"That we're finally going to have a real revolution in this country, hold our leaders accountable and that there aren't going to be any more oil wars. Things are heating up. The protest at the UN was a success. We have momentum now, but we have to keep pushing. We need you. Come on Myles, please give it another try? I know you could use the money."

The train was slowing as we approached the Middletown station. My grandfather was standing outside on the platform, rocking back and forth on his cane. His old bones shuddered when he summoned the strength to stretch a smile across his wrinkled face.

"I'd invite you to dinner tonight, but Sol is so sick," I said, gathering up my bags. "I don't want to overwhelm him."

Ari smiled when he saw the old man. Then he stood up and patted me on the shoulder. "No problem," he said. "I have to get back to New York tonight anyway."

"When will I see you again?" I asked, offering a handshake.

"I guess that's up to you, Myles," Ari replied, his voice changing to a whisper. He'd arranged himself to block the exit. "In case I wasn't clear: We need your help, now, more than ever. Either you're with us or against us. Do you understand? You have to decide."

"Do something to sweeten the deal," I suggested, anxious to push past him and exit the train. "I'm humbling myself a lot if I go back to your group. How do I know it's not another test?"

Ari liked my logic.

"You want a gesture of friendship? Is that what you want."

"That would be a start."

"Fine. You name it. Anything. I'll see that it gets done. Then we'll move past this misunderstanding and start to trust each other again. What do you say?"

"All aboard" The conductor called. I had to think fast.

"Can you pick up some white paint next Friday, and bring along some rollers?" I asked, rushing to the back of the car. "There's a job I have to do."

1:13 A.M.,
Thursday, March 6, 2008

I was sweating the whole subway ride downtown. I couldn't believe I'd brought a gun on the train. What was grandpa thinking when he left me that Luger in his will? I remembered the last time I saw him alive. We were sitting in the kitchen of his Jersey home. I told Sol about my conversation with Ari on the train, and how I'd wronged my friend when I slept with Melissa. Sol stroked his chin, thinking through all the chapters of his life.

"You've got to right this," he advised. "Stick to your friend. It's the right thing to do. Before the war I had a friend from Germany," he then explained his logic. "No matter who I killed over there, they all had the same face. I was always shooting at my comrade."

Desperate to find cell phone service and call Hailey, I held my phone out in front of me, sprinted up the stairs and through the turnstiles. Then I was smack in the middle of the city.

"Myles!" Hailey called, running toward me. She looked awful. Her hair was a mess and her skin was pale. "What's your plan?" she demanded, out of breath.

I glanced around, trying to remember the map that Professor Murphy had drawn of Times Square, showing each man's assigned position. The streets weren't packed anymore, as I'd seen earlier on the web-cam, but plenty of people were still wandering around.

"I think he was supposed to wait at the Hard Rock Café," I said, pointing across the street. Hailey took off in that direction. I chased after her. We plowed through the doors, past Paul McCartney's "Let It Be" bass-guitar and ran downstairs to the bar.

The bartender was wiping the counter.

"Have you seen this guy?" I asked as Hailey dug a picture of Ari out of her wallet.

"Yeah, I remember him," the burly man answered, adjusting his mane of gray hair. "He must have sat here almost three hours and only ordered one beer."

"Are you sure?" I asked, thinking that didn't sound like Ari.

"That's definitely him. He even told me his name. Around 11:00, he paid up, went out for a cigarette, then he came back and stayed another half-hour."

"Did he look alright?" Hailey asked.

"Lady, I'm sorry. Is that your boy?"

Hailey nodded.

"Look guys, I have to close up. Your friend was here forever. I've never seen somebody sweat over a beer like that. His eyes were red. I thought he'd been crying. He kept mumbling to himself, stuff about some professor. Anyway, some other guy came in around eleven thirty, maybe twelve? They left together."

"What did he look like?"

"Don't know. He was young. Fair-haired? They took a shot together and left a big tip."

"That was the last you saw?" I asked.

The bartender nodded and resumed his work. I looked at Hailey.

"What do you say?"

"Dylan?" she asked.

"Must be."

We went back upstairs.

"You decide where we go next, Myles. I'm all nervy," Hailey said when we were outside in Times Square again. I bummed a cigarette off her and tried to remember places where my friends would hang out.

Mistakes
(November 2007)

The day Hailey arranged for me to come and teach music class at the preschool, I would never have known that she and Ari were in the biggest fight of their lives. The experience was beautiful. The high-rise school was on 45th and First, about a block from the UN. I expected teaching to be as frightful as speaking at one of Miriam's impromptu poetry slams or prose readings, but then the children and their smiles set me wonderfully at ease.

"This is Mr. Myles," Hailey said, introducing me to the children she'd gathered in a circle. "He's going to play us some songs."

As I played tunes from my childhood, I realized city life had taken its toll on me. I'd grown bitter and impatient. Was my youth gone? Certainly my desire for fantasy was limited. Yet, these children were the opposite. Their minds were wildly imaginative.

After the music, I sat down at the art table and drew some of my pastel scribbles for the kids. I was embarrassed when Hailey pinned my picture up on the cluttered classroom wall along with all the other children's drawings, but she dismissed my complaints.

"Admit you're having fun," Hailey teased. I nodded, but grew increasingly pensive the longer I stayed there, admiring the children. A strange feeling had crept up in my gut. For the first time I could remember, I was genuinely interested in having a child. When Hailey prepared a snack for the kids, I let my thoughts slip:

"They're cute," I mumbled. "I want one."

Hailey was surprised. She turned around immediately. "Really?" she asked. We watched the kids munch on grapes and crackers. The room was silent except for their gnawing.

"Why not. Parenting could be fun," I said, trying to lighten the mood. But nothing worked. Hailey was caught up on what I'd said.

"If only Ari—" she started to complain, but stopped herself. Then she found her smile again. "I can't wait to have children," she said.

We went across the street for coffee when school let out. My treat.

"You're meeting Ari later?" Hailey asked about our plans to paint Nathalie's apartment.

"If he comes," I answered, sitting down at the corner booth.

"He'll come. I know he's always excited to see you. He'll probably bitch about me, though. Promise me you'll tell me what he says?"

"Why would he be angry at you?"

"Let's just say it hasn't been easy lately. Ari is going through something, you know? He's sort of homeless. He moved all his things into his professor's apartment on the East Side. I guess the work has been intense lately, and he often stays overnight. He spends the weekends with me. I don't know what to make of the situation, he's always moody when we're together. Maybe it's my fault? He's so devoted to that ugly professor and here I am pressuring him."

"To get married?"

"A little," Hailey answered with a half smile, trying to hide the dimples in her cheeks. She seemed embarrassed confiding in me, and I thought she was relieved when they called our number at the counter. When I came back with our coffees, I was ready to change the subject. Hailey, however, picked up right where she'd left off.

"I want to know he's serious about us. That's all. Lately he disappears," she explained.

"Do you want me to talk to him?" I offered.

Hailey shook her head. "Do you know anything about this 'Big Echo' game?" she asked.

"Of course. That's Ari's invention. Each player gets two minutes to speak extemporaneously."

"I know the rules. You've played?"

"I have. The game is fun. I think it needs a better name though. How about calling it *Monologue?*"

"Monologue. Big Echo. Whatever. The game has to stop. Every time we have a fight, that's Ari's solution. He says it helps us get our grievances out in the open, but I think it's pathetic."

"What are you fighting about?"

"Everything. Myles, it's awful."

The angst spilled out of her. They were having a real crisis. Ari hadn't been the same since they'd returned from Ireland. They'd had a great trip together, but now he was acting cold and bitter toward Hailey.

"I know it meant a lot to Ari to see his brother. He was hurt when Jeremy didn't come back with us, but why does he take it out on me? Now, Ari rails against the war every night.

He's so angry with the government. I hate feeling like I'm always waiting around for him to make up his mind what he wants in life."

I honestly didn't know how to advise her. Hailey smiled and finished the last of her coffee. "Walk me home?" she asked.

I didn't say no.

She kept her head down as we walked through Murray Hill. Since she wasn't saying anything, I opened up. Soon I was speaking my stream of consciousness in a sort of extended monologue, not realizing how much I was confiding in her.

"I really enjoyed the kids today. Did I tell you that already? I wasn't expecting to have fun. To tell you the truth, I was nervous. But I relaxed right away. I mean I'm such a kid myself. Look at me. Look at this hat. I look ridiculous, don't I? I go to the park—it's like Neverland. I play out all my fictions. I know I'm a fuck off. I'm not taking anything seriously, especially when I'm on a binge. That's how I lost Nathalie. Did Ari tell you what happened? I messed up. I really liked her. I miss her. Jesus, what am I doing? I don't know why I'm telling you all this. What do you care? I guess seeing all those children today put me in a mood."

"Can I ask you something?" I asked, but I didn't wait for Hailey to answer yes or no, the question blurted out. "How badly do you want children with Ari?"

Hailey shrugged and kept looking down. I breathed in her silence. The only thing I could think of to do was keep talking. I continued rambling, trying to understand their relationship with whatever words came to mind.

"I can imagine Ari's perspective," I said. "He's nervous, and he's scared. Having kids is a big step and a real commitment. Maybe he wants to accomplish something in his career first? Can you blame him? Of course it's hard in this economy. I know a lot of guys who feel stalled. The recession will deepen before there's a recovery. That's what everyone in finance is saying. There's bad debt everywhere. But money shouldn't matter. If you love somebody and you want kids, you go all the way, right? That's what I'd do if I were Ari."

"You would?" Hailey said, lifting her eyes off the pavement.

"Sure. Look at you, Hailey. You're smart, you're beautiful, and you've got your life together. You'll take good care of whomever you marry. If I were Ari, I wouldn't wait a minute."

She seemed flattered. We were at her apartment. I was about to say goodbye when she asked me to come upstairs.

"I should go."

"Please come up? There's something I want to show you."

We took the elevator to the third floor, and she let me into her two-person apartment.

"Where's your roommate?" I asked, hoping that someone would return soon to be a witness in case Ari asked about my day with Hailey.

"Work," Hailey replied, leading me through the living room. Her bedroom was too small for a desk or chair. She told me to sit on her bed and close my eyes. My heart was beating. I felt utterly out of place sitting on the white, flowery bedspread while she rummaged in her closet. I knew I was intruding again on Ari's intimacy. His things—clothes, toothbrush and pictures—were everywhere.

"Ok," Hailey said. "Now you can look."

I opened my eyes as she unfurled a large, black and white photo of Times Square.

"Did you take this?" I asked, approaching the poster.

"My friend works there. I took the picture from her office window on the 26th floor."

The perspective was interesting. Hailey had captured many faces in the crowd, but my honest opinion was that the work looked kitsch.

"I didn't know you were interested in photography."

"I went to art school. Ari always forgets. Tell me honestly, will Ari like it? I thought we could hang the picture in our apartment. That is, if we ever move in together."

I hesitated.

"You hate it, don't you?" Hailey said, growing defensive. "You're taking way too long to answer."

"The picture shouldn't be only black and white," I suggested.

Hailey stared at me as though I was out of my mind.

"You need to draw in the energy," I said, standing up from the bed. "Look at all these people. They're bland without any color. Surprise color and texture, that's what you need. Here:"

I went to my guitar case and brought out Chris' pastels.

"This is what we've been using to color on the wall," I explained. "I only manage to scribble, but I have fun. Drawing is so liberating. Color over the poster, that's my suggestion. Add in all the energy. Then Ari will love your picture."

Hailey looked at me and considered.

"Will you help me?" she asked.

I should have left right then and there. Touching that poster was a mistake from the beginning. We were scribbling over a perfect picture, destroying Hailey's heartfelt gift.

"Are you having fun?" I asked Hailey repeatedly. I was trying to measure her enthusiasm, but I hardly listened to her reply. I was on a creative tangent. "When I have kids, I'll let them draw on everything," I blabbered. "The whole house will be filled with their pictures. I'll play too. We'll stay up all night and never get tired. Just like my characters."

I was in my element, but I didn't realize how my fun was hurting Hailey. Suddenly she threw down her crayon. She was on the verge of tears.

"Stop, Myles. Please," she begged.

I took a step back. "You don't like it? The poster looks great," I insisted.

"No. It's ruined. This isn't what I wanted," Hailey said.

There was nothing I could say to change her mind. "Do you want me to leave?" I asked.

Hailey nodded.

I gathered up my things and retreated. "I'm sorry," I said. "I only thought the picture needed more color. You're such a bright person, Hailey. The poster was gray. Please, it's my fault. Can you print another? I'll pay."

We were at the door. Hailey was drying her eyes.

"Some people actually want to grow up, Myles," she muttered as I stepped into the hall. "Did you know that? Not everybody wants to be a kid forever."

1:25 A.M.,
Thursday, March 6, 2008

I had a feeling we were being followed, but I didn't see Professor Murphy until the doors closed on the subway. He was standing behind the turnstiles, resting his hands in the pockets of his trench coat, his face ghostly white.

Hailey saw me shiver.

"We should change trains," I said.

"Why? Who was that?"

I didn't answer. By the time we got to 14th Street, I'd changed my mind. The hour was late and trains would be coming less frequently. The last thing I wanted was to wander the subway with Murphy on our trail.

"Myles?" Hailey said. "Let's hop off and take a taxi? You're scaring me."

"Good idea," I said.

We exited at Spring Street. As soon as we were in a cab, heading south, I checked my phone. I had missed several calls.

I listened to Miriam's voicemail first. "Myles," she said, "I hope you have money left for a cab. You need to come here immediately. I'm at Lehman Brothers. The guard will let you in. Hurry please."

Next, there was a frantic message from Lee. "Murphy's got Dylan," the kid yelled repeatedly. "He's got my brother."

Nathalie's voicemail frightened me the most.

"Myles! Where are you?" she cried. "Some man is here looking for you. He's banging on the door—"

I called Nathalie right away. No answer.

I looked at Hailey.

"Was it Ari?" she asked.

I shook my head.

"Driver, turn around please," I said, tapping on the glass. "Take us to the Lehman Brothers building, Forty-ninth and Seventh Avenue."

"Lehman Brothers?" Hailey asked. "Myles, it's almost 2:00 AM."

"Miriam is waiting."

"Miriam? Who the hell is that?"

"She's a friend. She'll help us."

When we got to Lehman Brothers, the guard rang up to Miriam and called the elevator. On the 20th floor, I knocked on Miriam's door. She cracked it open.

"Tell the girl to take a walk," Miriam whispered.

"Why can't she come in?"

"She won't want to see this."

Both Hailey and I had the same instinct. We barged through the door. I had to cover Hailey's mouth to muffle her screams. A man was hanging above Miriam's desk. He was spinning slowly. I knew the clothes, I knew the shoes, I knew that profile, and I knew that face. Dylan dangled, strangled by a noose.

Hailey was shaking in my arms, her hot breath making my palms sweat. Miriam took out a bottle of whiskey and poured two glasses. "I told you not to let her in," she scolded, taking a sip as she sat down in the swivel chair by the window. "Will you cut him down already?"

Slowly, I let Hailey shrink to the floor. When I let go of her, she pulled her legs tightly to her chest. Then she rocked back and forth, whimpering.

"What happened?" I asked Miriam.

"After you left, I checked my bank account," she answered. "A lot of my husband's money is missing. I needed his access code to view all the transactions, so I came down here."

I stood up on Miriam's desk, lifted my friend's cold, stiff body and untied the knot around his neck. Next, I laid him down on the desk and checked under his shirt. Miriam and I knew from the marks we saw that he hadn't committed suicide.

I found myself against the wall, gagging. Anger? Disillusionment? Remorse? Snap shot memories of both Dylan and Ethan, smiling, laughing, alive, flashed rapidly through my thoughts. I had no idea what I was feeling. In fact, I was numb.

"We should call the cops, Myles," Hailey whimpered.

"That's out of the question," Miriam shot back.

Hailey recoiled. She was slipping into shock.

"We have to take her somewhere," Miriam said.

Absently, I nodded my head. I couldn't think that fast.

"What do we do about the body?" Miriam asked.

"Where is the freight elevator?"

"Then what?" she asked,

"We'll get him in a cab, pretend he passed out drunk, then drop him in the river."

"Wasn't he your friend?"

"Do you have a better idea? I won't call the cops until I find Ari. Besides, you have some explaining to do. Why was my friend hanging from your ceiling? Who had his fingers in your account?"

Miriam looked out the window. Hailey kept sobbing Ari's name. For the first time it hit me that Dylan was dead. This was what murder looked like.

"Myles," Miriam said, staring out at the street twenty stories below, "I'll take care of the body. You worry about the girl."

"No," I said, standing my ground. "That's my friend here. Where's Murphy? How are you two connected? You have to explain."

"Don't ask me that."

I spun her swivel chair, forcing her to look into Dylan's strained red eyes.

"Who did this?" I shouted.

Finally, Miriam's cool broke. She realized she had to tell me her secret. "It's simple, Myles," she explained, pushing her chair away from the body. "This bank is going to fail. Six years ago we started a hedge fund with Jim and Murphy. We were betting on properties and debt. The investment wasn't sound but everybody was playing the game. We had to stay competitive. At first, we made a killing. Then I saw the risk and got out of the market. Everything would have been fine except my husband kept his shares, almost eight percent of the fund. When he disappeared last year, I inherited his mess. Now Murphy has his hands in everything. Your friend, Dylan, was doing me a favor. He said he'd salvage what he could before there's a crash. Last week I paid him to hack into the account, but there was a problem. He needed that access code I told you about. I was on my way down to help him, but Murphy got here first."

"Why didn't you tell me?"

"You don't understand, Myles. We're too big to fail. There will be a panic if people learn what trouble this bank is in. Nobody will get their money out."

"Is this any better?" I yelled, pointing at Dylan.

"I'm sorry, Myles. I would have told you. I didn't even know Dylan was your friend until your name came up the other day. I thought he was just another broker."

"No. I should have known," I said, backing away. I could punch someone. Dylan had been warning me about the strange accounting going on for weeks. There was evidence everywhere—the crash at Bear Stearns, Jim's wave of sell orders. These were only the first signs of trouble.

I needed to retch. The bathrooms were down the hall. I barreled into the men's room. Crashing to my knees, I vomited red goulash into the toilet. Then I heard heavy breathing in the stall next to me.

I cocked the Luger, took a deep breath and threw open the door.

Ari was sitting on the toilet. He was rocking back and forth, reading from a crumpled piece of paper.

I dropped the gun and snatched the paper out of his hands. It was the pact, bearing all our names and signed with blood. Chris and Dylan's names were already crossed off, indicating they were dead. Lee's name was next.

Ari Paints the Walls White
(November 2007)

I decided to walk home from Hailey's. Another mistake. I was five blocks from Central Park when the sky darkened, then opened up. I felt as though I was stuck in Hailey's gray photograph. Cold rain fell as if for spite, up and down, raindrops shattering on the sidewalk and drenching me up to my knees. Meanwhile, my cheap umbrella twisted and tangled with everyone else's as people walked fast, heads bowed, splish-splash through the puddles.

Finally, I ducked into the subway at Columbus Circle and boarded a one, local train. The platform was packed. There was a standstill when the doors jammed.

"People," the conductor's booming black voice came on over the loudspeaker. "Today is Wednesday. You have two more days of work. Try to keep it together. Don't push, don't shove, let's all treat each other Christian."

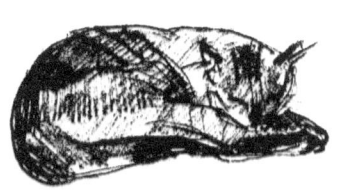

Boy, I would have loved to hear a monologue from that guy. He was mocking everybody. I pushed my way to the corner of the car and hung myself up to dry on one of the handles.

The college kid sitting next to me was dressed in a suit. He was holding a drenched résumé. "Work?" he said, forcing a laugh. "There's no work."

I nodded sadly. Things were spiraling out of control. Oil prices were spiking, markets were down, and banks were failing. I knew too many people who'd lost their jobs. First Dylan had called me up. He had twenty-four hours to clean out his desk at Bear Sterns. Then Alan got cut to part time. Lee had been peddling his résumé for months and Ethan had applied for unemployment. Even wealthy Jim and Sam were grumbling about the slowdown and the risky market. Nothing made sense. A popular theory of entitlement had left us stranded. The crash was imminent, and the crisis ran deep. My poor sick country, my tired friends. The bootstrap felt broken, and that broke our hearts. All we had ever tried to do was lift ourselves up.

Thank god for Professor Murphy, we were all thinking. He had our backs. When Dylan got sacked, Murphy found him something part time at Lehman Brothers. When Ethan was denied his veteran's benefits, Murphy doubled his handouts. The man guaranteed an apartment for Lee and cosigned on a loan for Alan. He was bankrolling everyone so long as the slump continued, and we paid him back with faith and loyalty.

When I got to my apartment building, Ari was standing out front, drenched, head to toe. The cans of paint he'd brought were stacked on the doorstep. The rain pattering against their lids sounded like tin drums. Poor Duke Ellington was scratching at the door.

"I was beginning to think I'd be homeless tonight," Ari said, waiting for me to find my key.

"You need a place to stay?"

"I can't stay at Hailey's. Not at Murphy's either."

The stray cat darted up the stairs in front of us. When I let Duke inside the apartment, he instinctively went straight to the radiator and curled up on the floor. Ari, meanwhile, approached the living room window and briefly scoured the street before he relaxed.

"You want some dry clothes?" I offered.

Ari nodded.

As I went to my room, I heard Ari rummaging in the freezer. When I came back, gin and tonics were sizzling.

"Hailey says I drink too much," he complained. "She says I work too much, too."

"Well, do you?"

Ari didn't answer. He went to the bathroom to change. When he came back, he used his pocketknife to pry open the tops of all the paints. I helped him move the furniture away from the walls. Then we spread out drip-blankets to protect the floor.

"You destroyed this place," Ari observed, amused by the damaged walls. "The men in your family sure know how to make a mess of things."

"What's that supposed to mean?" I asked.

"You and your dad are very similar, that's all. You both always have to go your own way. You like to have a good time at the party. Then you leave a mess behind."

"That's pretty harsh, Ar," I said, trying to stop him from going any further into the malpractice scandal that had ruined my father. Ari and I were in college when it happened. My dad was accused of stealing narcotics from the hospital where he worked with Ari's father. Even though it wasn't proven, Dr. Shultz never trusted his partner again.

"Speaking of your dad, you ever hear from him?" Ari kept prying, but by now I was on the defensive.

"I'm not going to answer that."

"Why not?"

"Whatever I tell you, you'll report to Murphy."

"Myles, please, you know I can keep a secret."

"Really? Then how does Murphy know everything about my dad? He knew about Melissa, he even knew about the girl I was seeing in Tel Aviv. You're the only one who could have told him all that."

"I never told Murphy anything," Ari insisted.

I didn't know what to believe, but Ari had reopened every scar. I was lashing out.

"Why did Murphy want to know about my father anyway? What does he want from me? And why do you keep me in the dark?"

"Calm down," Ari said, regretting the topic he'd chosen.

"Let's paint the damn wall already," I said, ending discussion.

For an hour, we kept our distance. Still, we were oddly in sync. Both of us were glad to have work with which to fill the awkward silence. Both of us were eager to finish painting so that we could have another drink and try talking again. I watched Ari make careful strokes with the rollers. He was as thorough as ever, but at times I noticed his thoughts were wandering. He clicked his jaw incessantly, preoccupied with the view from the window. Finally the tension dropped from his wrist, and he said what was on his mind.

"The place on 75th Street is being watched," he announced. "We all have to stay away this week. We thought it was the Feds. It's not."

"Then who?"

"Forget it. We're safe here."

Ari went back to the freezer and poured himself another twister of gin. He wanted to get drunk. I sat down at the counter and let him talk.

"I didn't mean that, before," Ari apologized. Then he praised my work for Murphy and the group. "All the boys are grateful," he said. "We're glad you came back."

"But you're in trouble?"

"I shouldn't be telling you this."

"What?" I asked, baffled. Ari was driving me mad. He kept letting me into his circle and then slamming the door in my face.

"You still don't trust me, do you?" I said. "That's what this is really about. You wouldn't have brought up my dad or said we're similar if you didn't want to make that point. But you know what? Forget it. I'm through with you and your group. You're right. I'm exactly like my dad. I go my own way. I've got no, what's the word?" I snapped my fingers, stuttering.

"Loyalty?"

"Right. No loyalty."

Shocked by my blunt confession, now Ari was conciliatory.

"Myles, you *are* loyal. I didn't mean that."

"Then what *do* you mean? I'm sick of beating around the bush, and I don't trust *any* of you. Especially Murphy."

"Believe me, I understand why you're skeptical. I didn't mean to insult you either. All I'm saying is that I think Murphy deserves to be shown something more than loyalty. You also have to believe in him. He's a good man. He's done so much for all of us already, and yet you refuse to have faith that he's sincere. Some of us worry that you aren't fully on our side, and I've been asked to watch what I say to you. I'm sorry, but it had to come out."

"Fine by me. Don't tell me anything. I don't need to know, and I won't be loyal or faithful to anyone. I'll take Murphy's money and write his damned propaganda, but it's only a job. I don't owe him anything."

That lit Ari's fuse. He turned around, furious. A big, echoing, monologue streamed out.

"How about being a part of something for a change? Would that kill you? Why can't you do something simply because it's good and right and helps your friends and countrymen?"

"You dragged me back into this, remember? I've done everything that's been asked of me since then."

"But you're passionless. Myles, you act as though you're a mercenary. That's why nobody can stand you."

"How *do* you want me to behave? Do you want me to pretend that I'm as angry as Murphy's soldiers? I didn't go to war. Neither did you. I'd feel fake."

"Are you telling me that even after meeting guys like Chris and Ethan you don't feel a little fucked up inside, a little angry and ashamed? Don't you feel responsible?"

I shrugged my shoulders.

"Jesus Christ, Myles, how about a little compassion? I know you were out of the country all that time, doing your soul searching, but you missed a hell of a show over here. The country has been going down the tubes for years already. The wars were a mistake and now the economy is going to bottom out too. Bush brought us to our knees. Don't you see what's happening?"

"Why are you shouting?"

"Because you won't understand, Myles. We need a change, a big change. I want to be a part of the change, not sidelined, choosing between swallowing debt or making bullshit money like the rest of the pawns and puppets in the government."

"And you think Murphy is the prophet of revolution?"

"He has the means."

"You've got delusions of grandeur. So far all I know is that you're jaded and paranoid that someone followed you over here tonight. Sounds to me like you're in over your head. You're not on the verge of any heroics."

"We're going to blow up the Army Recruitment Station," Ari was so worked up he blurted out the name of their secret mission.

Silence.

"What recruitment station?" I said, taking a step back.

"In Times Square. There is a little bunker right in the middle. You know it. Anyway, we're planning an attack."

This called for another drink—a kind of intermission. When Ari resumed his explanation, he spoke softer, conscious that he was spilling classified information.

"We've got seven men, not counting Murphy, Jim and Sam. They're only financing the operation. Some time this spring. That's when we'll strike. We already bought the guns and explosives off some drug cartel up in Harlem. That's who's been staking out the apartment. Murphy says he'll take care of them. Once we have everything safely stashed, we'll make final plans."

I was blown away. Ari was planning murder and destruction.

"I don't believe you'll kill anyone," I said.

"Kill?" my friend asked, staring strangely. "We're not going to kill anyone."

"Then why the guns?"

"They're for after the attack, in case there's chaos. The recruitment center is a symbol. That's why it has to go. We'll blow it up in the middle of the night after all the shows let out. Nobody will be inside then, but it will be a shock. Finally everyone will see the wars for a second."

"And then what?" I pressed.

Ari was prepared. "We'll have the whole city talking," he said. "Maybe even the whole country!"

"But you'll be terrorists."

"We're doing the right thing, Myles. The wars have to end. People have to see the truth."

His speech was endless. Ari went on listing American war crimes that sickened him and citing soldier horror stories. They were redundant arguments, but then Ari worked himself up to such a pitch that he started cursing Hailey.

"She doesn't listen. She doesn't understand. I try to explain the markets to her, how a real crisis is brewing. I try to explain how the wars have brought on the deficit and destroyed our image abroad, but she won't believe me. Her bullshit preschool optimism drives me mad."

"Stop it, Ari. Please stop," I begged him. "If the wars make you so angry, then let's not talk about them anymore tonight. Besides, you don't mean what you say about Hailey. It's just a rough patch, that's all. You're in love."

"I don't know anymore. I'm beginning to think she's naïve. Then, of all people, she goes and spends the afternoon with you? I didn't want to get mad about this, but she was crying when I called her this evening. What did you say to her? She wouldn't tell me what happened and I got jealous. I'm sorry. I'm venting. I don't mean to. Honest."

He was trailing off. All his angst and secrets were in the open now. We'd hardly reached a resolution, but at least we knew where we stood. Exhausted, we stared up at the walls. Somehow, the work was finished. The room shined white.

1:47 A.M.,
Thursday, March 6, 2008

"Nathalie!" I said, fumbling for my phone. "I forgot!"

Ari stared past me.

"Ari?" I asked before dialing. "If Murphy went looking for me and found Nathalie instead, would he kill her?"

"I don't know. Her name isn't here," Ari said, checking Murphy's hit list.

The phone was ringing. Nathalie picked up.

"Nat? Thank God. Where are you?"

Nathalie breathed and whimpered through a gag. Then the line went dead. A moment later I got a text message: "See you in the square."

I showed the message to Ari.

"What does this mean? Ari!" I yelled. "Chris and Dylan are dead. Ethan too, probably. Now Murphy has Nathalie."

"He's still going to attack," Ari muttered.

"The recruitment station?"

Ari nodded. "You were right, Myles. Murphy's been manipulating us. He's mad for power and we've fallen into his trap."

"We have to help Nathalie. Where would he take her?"

"He told you. Times Square."

"That's hardly a place to bring a hostage."

"He will."

"Then I'm going there."

"You're out of your mind. We're no match for Murphy. Unless we call the cops and turn ourselves in, Nathalie is as good as dead. The NYPD will find her. You know that, Myles. That's the best shot she has."

"What about Hailey?"

Ari looked up at me, confused.

"Your fiancée is down the hall. She saw Dylan."

Ari's face went deathly white.

"You brought Hailey?"

"She came by the apartment, looking for you."

"Is she alone?" he asked.

"No. She's with Miriam."

Ari wanted to hit me. Instead, he drove his fist hard into the wall, making a crash like cymbals. "You shouldn't have done that, Myles," he said, holding his hurt hand.

"She was upset, Ari. What else could I do?"

"Never mind. Tell Miriam to take Hailey to a hotel. I can't see her now. I'll go with you to find Murphy."

"What do we do with Dylan's body? He's lying on the desk in Miriam's office."

Something came over Ari. He could hardly speak. "I was too late to save him," he said, half to himself. Then he picked up my gun and pointed it at his head.

"Ari, don't kid around."

His eyes seized. He dug the pistol into his temple.

"Stop," I demanded. "Put the gun down."

"It's my fault," Ari answered shakily. "This is all my fault."

Winter Montage
(2007-2008)

The Great Recession was coming. The city's pace slowed as the gloom set in. The wet fall faded. The cold frosts stung. There was inflation. The streets seemed quieter during the day as people endured each new shock and prayed for their jobs. Was it a sign? One day I took a walk with Ari and Hailey through Central Park. The three of us were speechless when we saw the drained ponds and beggars scouring the muck for coins.

I saw pregnant women begging on the street. Garbage piled up. There was a fury in Murphy's meetinghouse when one politician announced that he thought the recession was merely "mental." The government's denial was shaping our common distrust. Hearts were hardening despite the talk of tax refunds, gas credits and bailouts. As far as Murphy's men were concerned, the market could dip, it could plummet. That didn't erase the fact that we were at war. There was no escaping the quagmire.

Then, at night, a strange and reckless release of energy took place in the city's bars. New Yorkers toasted the slump and drank away their troubles. Meanwhile, the conspirators gathered at Murphy's apartment. Gone were the days of the free-for-all parties. Frida dumped Dylan and left the group. Josie no longer came along with Ethan, and Alan broke up with his girl-friend. Only Murphy's lonely boys were left. There were eleven of us. We met on Tuesdays. Everyone would sit in the living room, grumbling about the worsening economy and the way it was distracting from the wars. We played Big Echo and drew on the wall, but games didn't help anymore. Our families were in trouble, and the boys were getting restless.

We marked up a map of Times Square. We held rallies and picketed outside the recruitment center. I had an editorial published in the New York Times about our work, but nobody was watching. All that mattered was the money flow to the banks.

Murphy had his ways of helping us. He gave stock tips and handouts, so that we could open up brokerage accounts. This worked out well, and we always made money, but we were poorly disciplined. In that atmosphere of peer pressure, nobody could enjoy anything independently. Whenever any-one scored a profit, they'd be forced to cash in their chips and support the group's endless binging.

Slowly, Murphy tightened his noose. His speeches echoed our bitterness. His kindness and generosity rendered us his servants. When Toto's closed, I had no way out. I had to dive into the work. I still owed over five thousand dollars in credit card debt and the interest was mounting. One by one we put our hands in to shake on the final pact and plot. We signed in blood, committing ourselves to the revolution. Our goal was to apologize to the world and to turn the nation around by force. It was going to be beautiful.

1:51 A.M.,
Thursday, March 6, 2008

The Luger rattled against Ari's skull. I froze.

"What did you say that night on Zoey's roof-top?" Ari demanded, shivering. "Remember your apology? You said, 'I'm sorry, I fucked up. Those were your words," he shouted as he kicked the toilet seat off its hinge. The whole thing came down crashing.

"Ari, I meant what I said," I tried to reassure. "I'm sorry."

"You're full of shit. Everyone is. Everybody is saying sorry now for something, and their apologies aren't worth a damn thing. How can any apology be sincere when there is no accountability?"

"Then hold me accountable, damn it! Hold me accountable for Melissa, for Hailey, whatever you want. We'll put this past us and forget. I'm sorry. Ok? I'm sorry I slept with Melissa. Put the gun down, Ari. Please?"

Ari's Monologue
(5PM., Wednesday, March 5, 2008)

"Before we're ever through all this, lots of folks will have to say: 'Sorry, I fucked up,'" Ari uttered one last monologue *before they all shook hands and departed for their mission.*

"This will be our apology," he argued between puffs on his inhaler and glimpses at his notes. "Tonight we'll do something right. Something no politician has managed. We'll say sorry for getting the war wrong and sorry for the mess we've made in Iraq. We'll say we're sorry for the tortures at Abu Ghraib and to the families of the soldiers who died over there. Tonight, we'll say sorry and end the war. We'll show the world that Americans *can* say sorry, and then maybe this country will be a happy place again."

Throughout those last quiet hours before their disastrous attack commenced, Ari had sought a way to forgive himself. He was reflecting on a confusing year. Maybe he had lost track of who he was? Certainly he was angry that he'd taken the easy way out when he joined up with Murphy. He knew he was a follower who had already followed most of the way.

1:55 A.M.,
Thursday, March 6, 2008

Drained and disturbed, my friend stood before me in a suicidal frenzy. Ari tried to break down his propaganda monologues. Somewhere, perhaps he'd find a reason to live? To begin, he knew he had to destroy his crooked symbols, his slogans, his rhythms and rhymes. He had to forget all his loyalties and cleanse his soul. But his voice was straining. He hardly knew himself. He had lost touch with time.

The clock ticked toward uncertain futures, through the loneliest, longest minute of my life.

1:56 A.M.,
Thursday, March 6, 2008

"Myles. I don't want this," Ari said, finally waking from his trance. "I don't want this for me and Hailey. I want to get married. I fucked up. I fucked up, too. Ok?" He said, fighting tears.

No. Ari wasn't suicidal. He put the gun down. We let it lay there for a few minutes.

Ari's breathing slowed down.

"Nathalie," we both remembered.

We sprinted down the hall and burst back into Miriam's office. Hailey couldn't believe her eyes. She rushed toward Ari, grabbed him and wouldn't let go.

"Dylan is dead!" she wailed, banging on Ari's chest. "Where were you?"

Ari hugged Hailey, smothering her shocked emotions.

Miriam put on her coat. "I'm leaving," she announced.

"You can't leave now," I said, stunned.

"My part in this is finished. The money is gone. You *will* take care of the body, won't you?" she said, already halfway out the door.

I dragged her back inside.

"How can you be so cold?"

"It must be my age."

I sensed the vacuum of her feelings toward me. "Where will you go?" I asked.

"The Caymans, Switzerland. I don't know. It's time I left. I never like the city in the summer. That's when the garbage starts to smell. Who knows, maybe I'll find my husband."

"Miriam, wait a minute. You won't ever be able to come back. There will be an investigation."

"You have no idea what's coming, do you? There's going to be a crisis. Nobody will kick up any fuss about a few murders and a missing widow when the banks crash."

"That's not going to happen. There will be a bailout."

Miriam didn't want a discussion. Again she started out the door. I caught up to her at the elevator.

"What should I do?" I begged her to help. "There's a girl—a friend of mine. Murphy kidnapped her. He'll kill her tonight if I don't find her in time."

"Forget the girl, Myles. Come with me," Miriam offered. "We'll go abroad. There's no other way out of this. You won't stop Murphy."

"I can't abandon Nathalie," I said, shaking my head.

The buzzer rang and the silver doors slid open. I held the door and barred the entrance. Miriam went stiff and tried to barge past.

"Let me go," she said. "Go save your muse already."

"Wait!" I pushed her back. The doors closed, but the elevator stood still.

"I warned you not to get involved with Murphy and his men," Miriam said.

"But you're a part of this too," I reminded her.

"No, Myles, your wrong. This was always my husband's gamble. I never played for the big money."

"Big money, small money. It all leaves a stinking trail. You're as guilty as I am."

Miriam watched me turn red. None of my antics moved her toward showing any sympathy. Cool and calculating, she was all business now.

"There are mail duffels in the closet down the hall. They're big. One should fit the body. The service elevator is around back," she said, checking her watch.

"You better hurry. The night janitor comes through soon."

I looked down the hall where she'd pointed.

"This is goodbye," Miriam concluded, pressing the button again. Then she pulled me close. Placing her dainty hand on my belt, she felt for the handle of the Luger. "Promise me you'll kill him?" she whispered, leaning close to kiss my cheek. "Kill Murphy."

The elevator doors opened. Miriam stepped inside.

"How will I find you when this is over?" I asked. Somehow that made her smile. "Publish the book already," she said.

The doors closed.

I was running on autopilot and adrenaline. No time to answer any of Ari's questions. I brushed past him with the duffel bag and scrambled about Miriam's office, cleaning up after the murder. Then I started packing Dylan inside the bag. When his cold limbs wouldn't bend, Ari got down on his hands and knees to help me. Hailey, meanwhile, was shivering. "You've got to take her home, Ari. She needs you. She needs to sleep. You both need rest. You have to help Hailey forget what she's seen. You're getting married, remember? Time to live. This madness ends tonight. Help me get Dylan downstairs, then I'll take care of Murphy."

At first Ari was reluctant to let me face Murphy alone, but gradually he agreed to my plan. We hoisted the duffel up over our shoulders. I grabbed Hailey's hand. Miriam's office disappeared behind us, the hallway blurred, the freight elevator dropped. There was a private parking garage below the Lehman Brothers building. We dragged Dylan to the darkest corner and hid the duffel in a cement crevice behind a parked car.

Outside on the street, I used the last of Miriam's cash to get them a taxi uptown. Hailey scrambled in first. Ari and I exchanged a hard, last look. We both knew it was goodbye.

"Don't stay at home tonight. Get a hotel. Get out of here as soon as you can tomorrow."

Ari promised he'd rent a car.

Like a couple of lost and lonely boys stranded on their jungle island, for a minute, I knew we both felt the Neverland spell. We were two old friends, wondering if we'd ever get to play again and could we have the same fun.

"Take care of yourself?" Ari seemed to say, but I wasn't sure. He was already inside the cab, and the door was shut.

Dazed, I stood in a puddle watching them drive away. Somehow I'd always known our friendship would end like this. We were more intrigued to discover how we'd finally say goodbye, than we ever were interested in making the friendship last. But this was a strange ending. My friend was gone, and it was up to me to save his happiness.

I started running toward Times Square. When I noticed the noise my shoes were making on the pavement, I slowed down and scanned every street corner for Murphy and Nathalie. I nearly tripped when a biker came up behind me, ringing his bell.

I watched the biker turn down the next street. Now I was expecting the worst. Maybe a sniper's bullet would pierce my skull, or else a blade would slit my throat. All I knew was that I was no match for the killer I pursued.

When I could see the recruitment station, I texted Nathalie. "I'm here," I typed. Then I ducked behind some scaffolding across from the bunker.

The time was 3:40AM. The street was quiet. Lights blinked. I could smell the first vat of coffee that one lonely street vendor was preparing. A few drunks staggered by. A taxi stopped at the streetlight.

My phone rang.

"Where's Ari?" Murphy snarled.

"He's gone."

"Show yourself!"

That was telling. Murphy didn't know where I was. I could bargain with him.

"I'll give myself up, when you let Nathalie go."

"There's no time."

"Murphy, don't hurt her."

The call clicked off. Suddenly that same biker I'd seen before emerged from the shadows. I couldn't see the rider's face, but for a second I thought I recognized Lee's bike.

The biker sped down the street, kicking up wet grit behind his wheels. He rang his bell again, this time as if to signal someone. Then he skidded to a stop in front of the recruitment station. I watched the biker dismount, run to the side of the building, unload a small box from the pocket of his trench coat and quickly return to his bike. The bell rang, and he sped off.

The blast came a moment later. That coffee vendor ducked. My ears popped. I felt the vibrations as though a fierce wind had struck my body. Metal and glass shattered. The air smelled like firecrackers.

I uncovered my eyes. There was a hole in the building. The poster of Uncle Sam was singed, framed by remnants of the glass window. Police sirens sounded. I spotted Murphy across the street. He held Nathalie by the wrist as he surveyed the damage with a flashlight.

Suddenly, Nathalie broke free. She bolted down Broadway. I called after her, foolishly revealing myself.

As Murphy charged toward me, I pulled out the Luger. I knew I was too shaky to take a clear shot. Thank God the sirens scared him. Murphy backed away, hiding in a shadow. The cops were coming from all directions. This was my only chance to run.

"West!" I shouted after Nathalie.

She kept running south.

I caught up with her when she twisted her ankle. Scooping her up over my shoulder, I carried her down the first quiet street I saw. Neither of us breathed again until we were at the Hudson.

6:43 A.M.,
Thursday, March 6, 2008

Nathalie slept as though she'd pricked her finger on a spinning wheel and succumbed to spells. She'd stir and breathe. At times, she opened her eyes in fright, but she was otherwise unaware of my presence, a sleeping beauty, paralyzed in slumber. As for me, I never got tired. The last hours of the night I sat by her bedside, watching the door with my gun.

To ease my nerves, I started the computer. Chatter filled my ears while I typed my story out. I could hear my friends talking, even Chris and Dylan, who were dead. I tried to transcribe their monologues, but I couldn't match their tones. The plot was agonizing. That mocking poet's voice always interfered. Every line I wrote came out heavy, swollen with descriptions that didn't do justice to their characters.

I'd made up my mind. It was up to me to kill Murphy. If I called the cops, then everyone would go down. Ari wouldn't have a chance to start over unless I killed Murphy myself. What mattered now was the novel. I had to finish. In case Murphy had followed us, I put Nathalie's desk in front of the

231

door to act as a barrier. Then I sat on top, writing the end. I'd raided Nat's purse. She had cigarettes and a canister of pepper spray. I kept them both nearby along with the Luger, puffed smoke incessantly, and typed away.

I was relieved to write the last line, "Never shall our hearts beat idle, not even in September," but I was soon overcome with paranoia. Watching the hallway through the peephole, inside I made certain that I had every corner of the apartment marked with the gun. Still, I feared how jumpy I was, and I couldn't master my breathing. Around sunrise, I gave up watching, tore off my clothes and climbed into bed with Nathalie.

She was in her underwear, hot as a stove. Delirious, she reached around and grabbed me. She was masturbating, and needed to come. She pulled me inside her. Squeezed, burned, tightened. Then she simmered, lingering in orgasm.

We lay in bed, wet with sweat. The slightest noises startled me. A creak in the floor, a mouse scurrying past, the traffic outside—I was constantly alarmed. What I really wanted to do was call up Ari, find out where they'd gone and if they'd heard anything about the murders. Unfortunately, my cell phone battery was low. I'd left my charger at Murphy's apartment. I figured it was better to text than to call.

Another hour ticked by. Ari never replied, and Nathalie slept on. When my face began to itch, I got up and looked in the mirror. I'd grown a beard. I checked the locks again. Then I went to the bathroom to shave and shower.

Beautiful white lights, speckles formed all around me as a migraine commenced. The water traced my embarrassing outline. I discovered bad skin, sharp ribs and wasting muscles. No big surprise. I knew I hadn't been taking care of myself. I wasn't eating right. My drinking and smoking were out of control, and I hadn't slept in days.

Feeling as cowardly as I'd judged Lee when he first showed up at the apartment earlier that night, I wanted to call my mom and tell her I'd shape up. But then I was ashamed. My grandfather had passed away, and I had missed the funeral. She had practically disowned me.

I made eggs and coffee for breakfast. Where were my senses? Nothing smelled, and everything tasted like chalk. I bootlegged an Internet connection and read the Times Online. There was *some* good news. The headline read: Blast Damages Times Square Recruiting Station. The subways around Times Square were shut down, and there was a picture of the broken glass surrounding that poster of Uncle Sam. That was about all they had on us. As far as I could tell, the authorities were already on the wrong track. I had dodged a bullet. That coffee vendor saw the biker flee, but he missed my standoff with Murphy. A manhunt was underway. No arrests had been made, and no bodies had been found.

I put on music—something jazzy—while I printed two copies of the manuscript. Then I started cleaning out my room. I deflated my mattress, swept the floors, threw out most of my papers and packed my bag. I hated taking down all the pictures and posters I'd hung up over the year, especially when I found that blue ball on which Ari had drawn Murphy's address. I didn't want to say goodbye to New York.

Finally, when the place was in fairly good shape, I sat down in the kitchen and mulled over the last questions I still had, pieces of the puzzle that didn't fit together. First of all, how could Murphy have kidnapped Nathalie at the same time that he was murdering Dylan? There couldn't have been more than twenty minutes between Lee and Nathalie's phone messages and yet the kidnapping and the murder had taken place on opposite ends of town. Besides, hadn't Hailey and I seen Murphy in the Times Square subway station? And who was on that bike? What motive did that person have to carry out the attack?

No way could Murphy have managed everything himself. There was an accomplice.... I considered a dozen possibilities before I determined that my work wouldn't be finished unless I got Murphy to talk. I'd have to corner him somehow, torture him until he revealed all his cronies. Then I'd pull the trigger.

Nathalie moaned, rolling onto her stomach. I rushed to her side.

"Nat, tell me what happened. I'm going to kill him. I promise. Who was he with?" I asked. "What did Murphy want from you?"

Nat's eyes opened and closed. She said nothing.

My phone rang. It was Ari.

"I might lose you," I said, warning him that my battery was weak.

"Don't worry. I can't talk long."

"Where are you?"

"We're in Binghamton, stopped for breakfast. I rented a car."

"Sounds windy."

"I'm outside. Needed a cigarette."

"How's Hailey?"

"She's fine. She's in the bathroom. Listen, Hailey thinks Dylan killed himself. Myles, I don't know what to do. I keep lying to her."

"Does she believe you?"

"I can't tell. But it gets worse. She knows I'm paranoid. Murphy keeps sending me texts. He sent me pictures of Alan and Ethan. They're both dead. He slit Alan's throat. Ethan's face is covered in blood. He's got all the bodies piled in some abandoned room."

"At the apartment?"

"No. That's strange too. He sent me a link. Somehow Murphy managed to get the apartment cleaned out last night. He's already listed it for rent."

"What about Lee and Landon? Any word?"

"Nothing."

There was a chime.

"Shit. Murphy's texting me again," Ari said. "He wants to meet. In public. He's called a truce."

"Where?"

"Central Park, at the entrance to Strawberry Fields. Some bench across from the Dakota. He'll be there at noon."

This time my phone beeped. The sound quality of the call was rapidly deteriorating as the battery wore down.

"I'm going to lose you, Ari. Text Murphy back. Tell him you'll be there."

The line went silent as Ari realized my plan. "You don't need to do this, Myles," he said. "It's my responsibility."

"No. I want to do this."

"How?"

"I won't get a clean shot unless we meet in public."

"You're out of your mind. The cops will pin you in seconds. I should take the fall for this. Not you."

"Ari, it's no use. I'm going. Text Murphy back. Tell him you'll meet him. I'll be there."

"Shit. Hailey's coming back."

"Good. Tell her whatever you have to. She loves you. I know she does. I want you guys to have a chance."

My ears were ringing as though another bomb had gone off. The piercing beeps of my phone combined with Ari's heavy breathing were unbearable. Finally, the call cut out. Ari never said what he'd decided to do, but it didn't matter. I had all the information I needed to go after Murphy, and I trusted Ari not to leave me high and dry.

I checked my watch. I didn't have long. What a bitter taste. I'd made up my mind to commit murder across the street from where John Lennon, symbol-man for peace, had lived.

I put on a Beatles record to pass the remaining time. Then I went to the closet and found that gray suit Jim had lent me. I got dressed and grabbed my fedora off the kitchen counter. There: I tied that tie, I tipped my hat. I stuck the Luger in my trousers. When I looked in the mirror, I was shocked. In that costume, I was someone else.

At 11:20 I wrote a hasty note on a post-it for Nathalie:

"For you, in case. Sorry. Love, ~Me"

I stuck the note to my manuscript and left the stack of papers by her bed. I put the other copy in an envelope, addressing it to Miriam's office. The record was still playing when I got ready to leave. Now I tasted spite. Finally, I could answer Murphy's question about the Beatles. No, I didn't believe in their music either. New Yorkers lead the loudest lives of desperation and nothing is going to change their world.

I looked out the window, thinking, God? Killing Murphy will set Ari free, won't it? Then Ari can marry Hailey, Nathalie will wake up, and I'll say sorry. But I found no guidance. I closed the blinds and looked through Nathalie's bookshelf. Authors and historical figures weren't inspiring. All my heroes *were* dead. In America, the Greatest Generation is passing. When my grandfather died, I thought there was nobody left to look up to.

I planted one last kiss on Nathalie's forehead and brushed her wet hair. She barely moved. I grabbed my bag, turned off the lights and said goodbye, locking the door behind me.

I dropped my package for Miriam in the mailbox outside Nathalie's apartment and started toward the subway on West 103rd Street. Everyone stared at me. The old Mexican lady who ran the laundromat on the corner came out to say "hola," but she was frightened when she saw my face. Those chess players looked up from their games and watched me cautiously. Even Duke Ellington came out to stalk me. Perhaps he sensed my evil? When I bent down to pet him, the old cat darted away. Then he watched me from the top of the stairs, hissing and growling as I went down to the subway.

I turned the corner and felt the wind of a coming train. How poetic. Beyond the turnstiles, there was a raggedy old beggar man playing "Let it Be" on his guitar. Morning light and soft white flower petals fell through the grates on the street above, announcing spring throughout the subway. Friends of mine were getting married, and I was on my way to kill a man.

-New York-Tel Aviv-Baltimore,
2008-2012

Credits:
(A Toast)

Cheers: Wes and Emma, who were both there and will be again... Joanne, who led me to New York and coached me along the way... Steph, who always calls it what it is... David whose poems inspire mine... Jake, who lends a line now and again... Arthur Magida, who showed these pages the razor's edge and left the appropriate trail of red... Bob Mrazek, my mentor and encouragement... Josh and Nanne, who have always supported my day dreaming... Diana, whose illustrations bring so much energy to my projects... Dara, whose photography embraces Myle's world... Dan, who shot the trailer... Ben, who leapt into character, enacting the pivotal scene... Blake, who always appreciates a dirty joke... And, of course, Avi, who dares to read my rawest words, and tells the hardest truths. Her cover design bookmarks our journey together these last five years when the book was always present.

Cheers: Papa Max, wishing you all the "Spice of life."

About Monologging.org

Traditional books have only one entry point. Websites, on the other hand, present countless portals. From links scattered across the web, readers are transported into the heart of a story when they visit Monologging.org.

Founded in 2011, the "local-global collaborative magazine" and press provides up-and-coming writers and artists with a platform to experiment and collaborate. Uniquely, the premise for Monologging.org derives from my novel, *All the Lonely Boys in New York.* The speaking game, "Big Echo," later called, "Monologue," helps the veteran soldiers portrayed in the book employ free speech and to overcome PTSD-related inhibitions.

For aspiring authors, this is also an excellent writing prompt. By evoking "Monologue" and other interactive models for intensive, two-way, creative communication, Monologging.org seeks to build an international community of writers and artists and to provide a social context for their work. Few experiences are more valuable to a writer or artist than seeing their creations indulged and re-imagined by a contemporary. Collaboration enlarges the scope of the creative works on Monologging.org, establishing a borderless realm for artistic projects.

In addition to great fiction and poetry features, the publication provides weekly arts-related reporting. However you've stumbled across Monologging.org, be it by print or by click, we hope that the collected media has enhanced your reading experience, inspiring you to connect.

-Jeffrey F. Barken